# HEARTS ABLAZE

## FORGED IN THE CITY

### A.D. ELLIS

*A big thanks to Cliff!*

# 1

## CHASEN STEELE

*QUACK, quack.*

I watched as the noisy water fowl made their way toward me, hungry for the duck food I'd bought from the vendor. I soaked up the sun as I stood at the little pond in a park just off Massachusetts Avenue in Indianapolis.

Fall in Indiana was gorgeous. Thanks to my time in the Army, I'd lived in quite a few locations, but I always felt like Indiana did fall best.

I'd come to Indianapolis that day to look into jobs since my most recent place of employment had, once again, not worked out.

Eight years in the Army had not worked out as planned. I'd planned to make it a career, be a lifer. I'd started as a grunt and worked my way up.

And then I fucked up my knee. Medically discharged after a grade two ACL injury. I was able to avoid surgery, but the injury earned me a ticket out. Although, I did get a small monthly payment that at least helped with groceries and a couple bills.

After recovering from the injury, I immediately began the hunt for a place to stay and a job. I lucked out with a somewhat decent apartment far south of Indianapolis. The roommate situation was tense, and likely wouldn't end up being a long-term thing, but the rent was cheap and I landed a pretty good job fairly quickly. But that didn't last.

I was now out of a job for a third time thanks to companies going under, changing to remote work—which I wasn't set up for in my current rental situation—and losing a position because I was the newest on staff. Last hired, first fired.

So, I was in Indianapolis on a beautiful, breezy fall day looking for a job and decent place to live. Maybe school. The Army was paying for classes, but every time I got ready to register or start classes, I lost a job and had to worry about a new one and making rent. For the time being, school was getting pushed off at least a semester or two.

"You gonna keep teasing those ducks or actually feed them?" A deep voice to my right startled me from my thoughts.

I jerked my head to the right and found dark hair, dark eyes, and a smirk. Glancing down at my handful of duck food, I looked to the pond and saw the ducks were not so patiently swimming around and scolding me. "Shit, got lost in my own head, I guess. Sorry, ducks." I tossed the food into the water for them and smiled slightly as they gobbled it up.

"Pretty sure they get fed plenty, but I started to wonder if they were going to come nibble your shins if you didn't give them their food." He smiled as he crossed heavily tattooed arms in front of his black t-shirt covered chest. "Ducks can be mean."

"Nothing like the geese, though." I shivered.

"Geese are nasty motherfuckers," the guy agreed with a genuine smile that crinkled the corners of his dark eyes.

I laughed. "I wonder how they keep the geese away from here? I'm surprised they haven't overrun the ducks."

He shrugged. "Who knows. Don't question it. I come here on work breaks sometimes, I *do not* want to have to deal with geese. No goose poop, no hissing, no chasing, no honking."

My ears perked up. "You work around here?"

"Over at Whitfield's Motorcycles Sales and Service." He threw a thumb over his shoulder to indicate the direction of his place of employment. "Just started there about six months ago. You looking for a job?"

I sagged slightly. "Yeah, definitely looking. But I know next to nothing about motorcycles. I mean, I can drive one, but nothing about selling or fixing them."

"I think there's quite a few places hiring around here if you're not against manual labor or food service." He seemed to empathize with my job hunt.

"Fucked my knee up in the Army, can't do a ton of *heavy* manual labor I used to be able to do, but I can do a fair share and I'm not against any kind of work at this point. If it pays my rent, I'm in." I looked back at the ducks before turning to the man again. "You got a place around here?" When he nodded, I continued. "What's the rent like?"

He winced. "Well, I think my landlord lets me pay a little less than what he could probably get for the place. But the apartment is above the shop. It's small, but it's nice. I think most places run anywhere from about $550 to $1200, with the average around $1000."

I nodded. "Yeah, that's about what I've been thinking. Guess I'll need to nail down the job first, then figure out the living arrangement."

"Where you living now?"

"Way down south of town. Rent is *cheap*, but so is the living space. And my roommate is kinda an ass." Although, I should have been grateful he let me borrow his car. Speaking of which, I needed to finish my job search and get Todd's car back to him. "Well, I better get going. Lots of applications to gather."

He pulled out his phone and checked it. "Yeah, I need to head back to work. Glad I was able to help the poor ducks survive you." He winked before turning to leave.

My heart fluttered.

What the hell?

My heart *fluttered*? From a guy I just met—didn't even know his name—winking at me? I rolled my eyes and watched him walk away. What the hell was I doing? I hadn't noticed a guy's ass since high school, and I'd proven to be as shit out of luck in the romance department as the job department. Male or female didn't matter. In my defense, I hadn't done a lot of dating.

I'd been on my own since I was eighteen. Before that, being attracted to girls—or that one guy in my Gym class —and dating had been awkward and distracting. After I left home and joined the Army, I really didn't have the time for dating even if there had been interested parties.

So why was I checking out a stranger's ass? My sexuality wasn't something I gave a lot of thought to. I'd spent so much time drowning at home, then enlisted and deployed, and now just trying to survive, that I didn't have much left to give to a relationship.

Did I find girls attractive? Sure.

I frowned.

Did I find guys attractive? I had to think about that for a moment. The guy in high school—who, at the time, I chalked up to looking up to an upper classman—maybe a couple of friends or acquaintances in the Army, and now this guy.

So, yes.

But it didn't matter. I needed a job and a place to live. I needed to figure out what the hell I was going to do with my life. I didn't even know his name and we'd met at a park in a city of almost 900,000; I'd probably never see him again. So, finding him attractive, even if it meant kickstarting a bisexuality I'd pushed to the back of my mind, was a moot point.

I was alone. I'd been alone since I was eighteen. Who was I kidding? I'd been alone for a long time before that. Thanks to a shitastic mother—who may have been dead by now for all I knew and cared—I had no family; at least no family who knew where I was. After being required to leave the Army, I didn't have friends around. No job meant I didn't have coworkers. All I had was a sketchy roommate who didn't like me, and a rent payment that needed paid. I ran my fingers through my hair and sighed before reaching in my pocket. I had just enough change for a soda and one more serving of duck food. And then I *had* to go get more applications.

\* \* \*

I gave the greedy ducks the last few pieces of food before sipping the last of my soda and tossing it in the trashcan. I glanced around the park trying to get an idea of which direction I should head as my phone buzzed with a text.

*1-317-555-0102: This is Virginia South. I'm trying to reach Chasen Steele. If this is Chasen's number, you'd know me best as Aunt Ginny. I have some very important information to share with you. Can you please reply and let me know if I've found the right number?*

I stared at the phone screen for what seemed like forever. *Aunt Ginny?* I'd loved her so much. She'd been the only family I had aside from my mother. Aunt Ginny—my mother's much older sister—was a flight attendant nearing an early retirement when I was younger and she only came to town a few times a year. But, when she was around, Mom was nicer and we always had a good time. I often wanted to catch Aunt Ginny alone and tell her about the shit Mom did, but then I'd feel guilty about putting her in the middle of it. Sometimes I wondered how my aunt didn't recognize that Mom treated me like shit and was almost constantly under the influence. But Ginny—on a strict flight attendant's schedule—always gave Mom a day or two notice that she was coming to visit, so Mom would clean up, throw away the trash, hide the pills and bottles, and send me for groceries. I loved when Aunt Ginny came because we had actual food and not just cereal, frozen waffles, pizza, and canned soup. Mom was almost *nice* to me when her sister was around. I always cherished the few days of peace and the time I got to spend with my aunt.

When I left home on my eighteenth birthday, I didn't give a damn about leaving my addict, alcoholic, abusive mother, but I did hate to lose contact with Aunt Ginny. I left my phone—the crappy one Mom let me use only to call her and find out what she wanted me to pick up on the way home—the debit card mom had me use for buying groceries, her smokes, and alcohol. I didn't take the car because it was registered in her name. As far as I was concerned, I'd hoped Mom would think I'd dropped off the face of the earth.

But I did miss Aunt Ginny like crazy those first few years I was on my own. When others were getting care packages and mail in the Army, I watched longingly as they opened the boxes and crowed over the items they received. Luckily, most of the guys in my squad were great about sharing. But I always knew that Aunt Ginny would have sent kick-ass care packages.

What could she possibly have to tell me? A ball of tension grew in my belly, but a sincere curiosity buddied up to the apprehension. I thumbed in a reply.

*Me*: *This is Chasen. Chase. You found me.*

As I waited for her reply, I put her name in my phone. My heart warmed with the thought of having *someone* to talk to. And her number was a 317-area code, so she was likely living in Indianapolis. Mom and I had lived in a tiny little town in southern Indiana when I was younger, but Aunt

Ginny had always talked about loving Indianapolis and how she loved when she'd get layovers there so she could enjoy the city. What were the odds that Aunt Ginny and I both had gravitated toward Indy despite having no clue where the other was located?

*Aunt Ginny: I've been looking for you for so long. Where do you live? Is there any chance you could come to Indianapolis? I can help a little with a plane ticket or gas money.*

I blinked at the screen and laughed before running a shaking hand over my face. Aunt Ginny was in Indianapolis. It was quite possible that I was only minutes away from her. Fate seemed to be working overtime today.

*Me: Believe it or not, I'm actually in Indianapolis right now. Do you want me to come to your place? Give me the address.*

## 2

# ALEXANDER "XAN" COPPERFIELD

AS I LEFT THE PARK, I fought the urge to turn around and check the guy out again. In my thirty years, I'd never entertained the attraction I had toward guys—based on how I grew up and the crowd I got in with, it would have been a dangerous situation—but that didn't mean I couldn't appreciate a hot guy when I saw one. And the blond guy feeding the ducks at the park definitely fit the bill for *hot*.

He was about two inches shorter than my 6'1", pale skin, light ice-blue eyes, pale blond hair in a style that was reminiscent of his service, and a killer smile, even though he seemed deep in thought and frustrated. *Damn*, I knew the feeling. Seemed like *worried* and *frustrated* had been my theme words for as long as I could remember. But I got glimpses of the stranger's smile a couple times, and I stupidly had the urge to make him smile all the time.

"You're an idiot," I mumbled to myself as I walked toward Whitfield's. "You didn't even get his name." Not to mention, the guy hadn't been giving off any *interested* vibes, so I needed to just stop that train of thought.

*Would you even recognize if a guy was giving off* **interested** *vibes?*

I pushed the thought away as I entered the shop and breathed deeply. A mix of scents hit my nostrils as the essence of the sales floor and repair bays mingled on the air. Leather, oil, rubber, gasoline, wax, paint, and the popcorn Bay Whitfield, my boss and the owner, kept popped for employees and customers alike. Most shops I'd worked for in the past would have had a musty smell mixed with beer, cigarettes, and weed. But Bay ran a very tight ship. Alcohol and pot were a major no-no on the job. Bay wasn't against his guys partaking off the clock as long as they didn't let it come to work with them or cause any problems. Cigarettes, vaping, tobacco of any kind were allowed, but not inside. Smoke breaks were allowed out back of the shop.

The day I walked into Whitfield's looking for a job, I nearly turned around the moment my eyes adjusted to the indoor lighting. No way a place like this would hire a guy like me. But, before I could hightail it out the door, a sexy silver fox—probably early fifties—smiled and headed my way.

*"Welcome to Whitfield's. I'm Bay Whitfield, the owner. What can I help you with today?" Even in a black t-shirt and worn work jeans, Bay had a commanding presence and put me at ease somehow.*

*I cleared my throat. "Um, Alexander Copperfield. Xander to most, Xan to some." I stuck my hand out to shake. "I've worked with motorcycles since before I could even legally drive. Wondering if you've got a need for a mechanic?"*

Bay's brow rose. "You any good?"

I nodded. "One of the best."

Bay cocked his head. "Let's go to the repair bays. Take a look around."

We walked through the large, open garage-type door between the sales floor and the shop. At least twenty bikes were in some state of repair or detailing. Various makes and models were lined up neatly in separate bays or sitting off to the side. My heart thumped at the thought of getting to work with these beauties every day.

Motorcycles were what I knew. My dad left us for his "real" family when I was small. Then my mom left me. I ended up as a ward of the state and spent year after year after year in foster homes. Despite the great stories that come from foster care from time to time, I did not experience the good side of the system. I spent most of my time wandering the streets, no matter what shitty house I'd ended up in that month, and always gravitated toward motorcycle shops, guys working on their bikes in their driveway, bike enthusiasts meeting in parking lots, and motorcycle clubs. I couldn't remember a time I didn't have my hands elbow deep in a bike.

The chance to work on bikes was how I ended up with a really bad crew. They had me running drugs, stealing, and other illegal shit. But they also gave me free reign to fix the club's bikes, so I stayed. Until I couldn't stay any longer. Until I knew I had to do better for myself before I ended up no better than my parents. No better than the thugs I'd fallen in with.

I moved a couple states away and tried to start over. Had to change shops every three to six months for a while, and my last location had proven no better than the old crew, so I was in desperate need of a job.

Whitfield's would be a dream come true.

We stopped near an area where three men were working on bikes. I took in the array of bikes and nearly sighed at the sight. A Harley Softail standard, a Harley custom Fatboy, and a Big Dog Chopper with a gorgeous raked out front end. The guy in the middle turned to Bay. "Gonna fire this bitch up, tell me what you hear."

The Fatboy roared to life and the sound vibrated in my chest.

Bay and I listened for a few moments until the man raised his brow for an answer. Bay turned my way. "Got any ideas?"

I closed my eyes and listened for a few moments longer. "Got the primary chain and valves tapping and smoke from the exhaust. Gonna need a primary chain tensioner, a valve job, and a ring job on your pistons." The words flowed from me as surely as my next breath. "If you've got the parts, I could repair it if you want to see me work."

Bay smiled and nodded. "Cliff, can you get started on the Honda that came in earlier? I'm pretty sure it's an easy fix, can probably have it done and out of here by the end of the day."

Cliff pursed his lips and looked me up and down. "Newbie?"

"Gonna test him out on this job. See if he's as good with his hands as he is with his diagnosing skills."

Bay showed me to the parts closet. Although, closet wasn't exactly the right word. The area was huge. He gave me a moment to take in the organization of the parts and then crossed his arms and waited. I grabbed what I needed from the closet and then headed back to the bike.

By the end of repair hours at the shop, I'd repaired the Harley and had it purring like a giant kitten. Bay slapped me on the back and smiled. "Come to my office. I've got some paperwork and some questions."

I couldn't help the grin as I ran my hand over the bike before shutting it off. I worried about the paperwork and questions, but

*I knew I'd impressed Bay and I'd had a hell of a great time doing it.*

*We settled in Bay's office and he tossed me a bottle of water. "So, I'll be upfront here. I'm going to ask a lot of really invasive questions. You can lie or dodge them, but in order to be hired, I'm going to run a background check. So, you may as well be honest about your past." He gathered a packet of papers. "I'm not going to deny you employment based on mistakes of the past. A lot of those guys out there," he pointed to the shop, "have less than stellar backgrounds. But they work hard, show up, do a good job, and respect me, my business, and my family. It's all I can ask. While I might not be thrilled to have some of them watching my eight-year-old son or infant daughter because of their lack of experience with kids, most of them I'd trust with my life, my children's lives, my husband's life."*

*My eyes shot to his. "You have a husband?"*

*Bay cocked a brow. "I do. We've been married about three years now. His name is Kyson. That going to be a problem for you?"*

*I swallowed thickly. "No, uh, not at all. Just never worked in a shop where a gay man could be out and proud and married with children and all that." I wanted to go on, explain more. Tell Bay that his sexuality and relationship being accepted at this shop gave me hope that one day I could date whoever I wanted and no one would give me shit. But I had a lot more to think about right then than dating. So, I kept it to myself.*

*"Most of the guys aren't throwing me a rainbow parade, but they respect me and know that I don't tolerate bigotry of any type." Bay smiled. "Plus, they adore Arlo and Cori. And Kyson won them all over with free sessions at his massage practice." He straightened the pages and clicked a pen. "So, tell me what brought you here."*

*I launched into a very open and honest tale of how I was the* result of an affair. My dad stuck around, mostly on weekends, until I was about two before he got fed up with Mom and left to devote his time to his "real" family. I could still remember what Dad looked like; I saw him every day when I looked in the mirror.

After about three years of drowning her sorrow in an ocean of Jack Daniels, my mom took off. Took me to a neighbor's, hugged me, and told me she was sorry and that she wanted so much better for me, and waved goodbye. She never came back. The elderly neighbor was in no position to care for me long-term, so I ended up in the care of the state.

Bay frowned when I told of the craptastic experiences I had in foster care. I shrugged it away. "Not all foster homes are bad. Guess I just had bad luck."

I crossed my arms over my chest as I told of my early involvement in gangs. Drugs, stealing, battery, sex, I spilled it all.

"You sold drugs? Did drugs?" Bay steepled his fingers under his chin.

I shook my head. "No, I was just their runner. I didn't even realize what I was running until I was much older."

"What did they have you stealing?"

"Mostly parts from rival shops and clubs." I shrugged. "I never really got in good with any of the crews because I moved so often. I was just a grunt."

"You harmed others?" Bay cocked his head.

I chewed on my bottom lip for a moment. "The last club I was involved with would do these fight nights. They'd pair up rival members and put them in the ring, bet on them, and let the fight go until one guy was out for the count or worse. They liked to bet on me to win; I usually did. They'd give me a tiny cut of the pot."

"Sex? Consensual?" Bay's jaw looked ready to pop.

I took a deep breath. "I was an early bloomer. Two of the crews liked that about me and let me 'earn my keep' with anyone willing to fork over cash or weed."

"Fuck," Bay bit out. "They pimped you out?"

I wrinkled my nose. "Yeah, in hindsight, I know that's what they did. But I was a teen with raging hormones. I got some money, they fed me, let me work on bikes around the clock, and woman were all over me from the time I was thirteen until I left around age twenty. At the time, I thought I was the luckiest son-of-a-bitch around. Most of the women were pretty young, I looked a lot older than I was, and I was just as eager for it as they were."

"That's a hard pill to swallow. Consensual, but under the legal age of consent. By definition, statutory rape." Bay blinked slowly and took a deep breath. "I'm sorry you were a part of that. Were you safe?"

"Yeah, that was the one thing that was always pounded into my head. They were involved in drugs, theft, and a handful of other illegalities, but condoms were a must. How weird is that?" I chuckled with no humor.

"Just women?" Bay frowned.

I swallowed thickly. "No way a guy could have paid for me without calling major attention to himself. And that definitely wasn't something a guy in those groups wanted to do." I stared at my shoes. "Didn't keep me from wishing some of the guys my age, a couple of the older ones too, would show some interest. Just wasn't something that happened. Not without major consequences."

Bay nodded. "I can see that. Well, Whitfield's isn't like that. We're legal in everything we do. No one has to do anything to 'earn their keep' and everyone is safe here no matter their gender or sexuality. I want you to know that. Whether you end up working here or not, this is a safe space."

My heart warmed and I sniffed away the sting of tears.

"What made you get out?" Bay scribbled a few notes.

*"Finally wised up. Figured out when I was about sixteen that they had me running drugs. Worked my way to finally being able to leave at twenty. I hightailed it out, crossed a couple state lines, found odd jobs here and there. Found temporary work with different shops. Couch surfed a lot, took advantage of hotels with weekly and monthly rates, and steeled myself to do honest work. I refused to turn out like my parents. Refused to be like the crews I'd fallen in with. Ended up in Indy by chance. Whitfield's was the name everyone mentioned when I asked about motorcycle shops."* My cheeks heated after the words spewed from me. *"Sorry, that's a lot of shit to take in."*

*"No worries,"* Bay said with a soft smile. *"You give your permission for me to run a detailed background check?"*

I nodded. *"Yeah. I got in trouble as a minor, but nothing on my adult record. Not sure how I managed that, but I'll take it. May find a couple speeding tickets. My credit isn't stellar."*

Bay slid a piece of paper across the table and I signed for the background check.

*"You got a place to stay?"* Bay asked.

*"Not yet. But the hotel I'm at isn't terribly far from here. I've got a bike for back and forth. I'm punctual and I'm a hard worker."* I liked Bay, I loved his shop, and my heart already hurt at the idea of not working here.

Bay put the papers in a folder. *"What would you think of taking a slightly lower salary in exchange for the apartment upstairs?"*

My eyes grew wide. *"For real?"*

He nodded. *"It's small and nothing fancy. But if you'd be willing to make a slightly lower salary and maybe help with shop clean up, keep an eye on things, the apartment is yours. Utilities are covered. You can use the cable and internet we use for the shop and sales floor. You'd basically just have to pay for your own groceries and toiletries."*

*I stared at him for what felt like an eternity waiting for him to laugh, say he was joking, or add in something nefarious. He didn't. He just waited. "Seriously? Like I could work here, keep the shop clean and looked after, live upstairs, **and** get paid?"*

*Bay smiled. "Assuming the background check doesn't raise any red flags, and you want the job, yes. Some of the guys only work evenings or weekends part time. Some of them have clients who request them. I'd be looking for you to work weekdays, mostly ten to six. Keep an eye on things since you'll be right upstairs. Weekends you can pretty much set your hours. And, as a newbie, you'll get whatever jobs others don't want. But based on what I saw you do with that bike back there, you'll be earning your own clients and top jobs in no time. No smoking, chewing, or vaping in the building. Weed is a big no onsite; don't care what you do offsite on your own time. No drinking on the clock." He cocked a brow. "What do you think?"*

*My head felt fuzzy and I nearly swallowed my tongue, but my face broke into a wide smile. "Yes, definitely yes. Where do I sign?"*

*A week later, I was moved into my new upstairs apartment and officially hired by Bay at Whitfield's Motorcycle Sales and Service.*

I smiled as I recalled the first day I met Bay. Checking the clock on the wall in the service area, and ignoring the teasing comments from some of the guys, I set about cleaning the shop floor, arranging tools, picking up trash, and even went to the retail stockroom to be sure it was organized.

"Oh, good. The maid is here. This place was looking like a pit," Jorge hollered from where he was working. He wasn't wrong, the guys *were* pigs for the most part, but I knew his comment was just in fun.

"Well, if you all would clean up after yourselves, I wouldn't have to be so picky with keeping this place looking good. Bunch of pigs. What do your own places look like? Disasters based on the way you junk this place," I teased as I swept.

I was pretty particular with keeping things clean. Maybe it was just my nature, maybe it was the filthy homes I'd been forced to live in, likely a combination of the two. Keeping things neat and tidy calmed me, gave me a sense of purpose, and kept me useful to Bay.

By six, I'd finished the clean-up and threatened bodily harm against anyone who messed it up. With a wave, I headed upstairs to shower off the grime that inevitably came with working in a motorcycle shop. I tossed my work jeans and black t-shirt in the wash and jumped into the shower as my stomach rumbled loudly.

I thought to the groceries I had in the apartment. Ramen noodles, frozen pizza, cereal, oatmeal, bread, milk. Beer, soda, water. I could also order pizza. I had food, I wouldn't starve. I shook my head and chuckled. Who was I kidding? I knew I'd end up at The Salty Lizard like I did almost every evening for dinner.

Bode and Sage Silver, owners of The Salty Lizard, had welcomed me with open arms when Bay introduced me to them six months ago. Actually, their whole group had accepted me. Bay's husband, Kyson, was one of the calmest, kindest people I'd ever met. Their kids, Arlo and Cori, were fucking adorable. Bode was Kyson's cousin. Bode was married to Sage—a fact that struck me as strange when we all first met because Sage looked younger than me by at least a couple years and Bode was definitely at least a bit older than me—and they had a little boy named Oliver. They had been foster parents for him at first, but he now belonged to them. Bode and Sage had just recently taken in Rosie, a little girl about seven who had the prettiest blonde curls and icy-blue eyes I'd ever seen.

The crew was rounded out by Bode's twin, Benji, and his husband, Rhys. Benji and Rhys had two great dogs, Bear and Brawn. I didn't get to see them as often as Bay, Bode, and Sage, but they were great guys.

If someone had told me six months ago that I'd be working a dream job, with a fantastic apartment, and six men and their families as friends, I would have laughed. But here I was. I had actual friends, a steady job, and a great little place to live.

Sometimes I got a little jealous of the guys and their happiness, but, for the first time in my life, I felt safe, peaceful, and stable. Maybe I was still missing that connection, the close friendship or relationship like the Silver crew had, but I was only thirty. If and when the right person came along, I was now in a position to form that connection.

A flash of sadness hit me as I thought of my parents. Was I destined to be sad and alone because of them? I shook off the melancholy and headed down to dinner at The Salty Lizard.

## 3

CHASE

ONCE AUNT GINNY sent me the address and I plugged it into my phone GPS, I realized I was less than thirty minutes from her. I stood and nearly ran to my car. Then I froze. *Shit*. It wasn't *my* car. Todd would be wanting it back. And I needed to get applications. I took a deep breath before making a split-second decision. *Fuck it*. I wasn't going to miss a chance to see Aunt Ginny after ten years. I stalked to the car.

Twenty-five minutes later, I checked the address and climbed from the car. I frowned and my stomach flipped as I walked into Rose Gardens assisted living. An antiseptic scent was only slightly hidden by a flowery one. A lady at the front desk looked up when I walked in.

"Welcome to Rose Gardens, how can I help you today?" She smiled.

"Um, I'm supposed to meet Virginia South?" I stumbled over Aunt Ginny's real name.

"Perfect. She said she was expecting a guest. Follow

me." The lady, Nicole as her name tag indicated, stood and gestured toward a door.

I silently followed her down a large main hallway. We reached a T; to the left and right were two smaller corridors.

"Ginny spent some time in our medical wing earlier today." Nicole gestured toward the left. "But she should be running game time by now." She pointed down the hallway on the right. "I'll show you to the community room."

I swallowed thickly. Aunt Ginny needed assisted living? What did she need in the medical wing? Was she sick? As I walked behind Nicole, I recalled Aunt Ginny as she was the last time I saw her. She was planning to retire from the airline at age fifty-five and then work at a bookstore or something similar. So, she was probably fifty-three when I left home. That would make her, what? Sixty-three? That wasn't old, not at all. What could she be doing in an assisted living center?

As we entered the community room, I heard laughter as Bingo numbers were called. I recognized Aunt Ginny's voice before I even saw her. And then she turned, her short, silvery white hair still as stylish as I remembered, and smiled as if I was a treasure she'd spent her life looking for. I walked toward her and soon I was engulfed in a hug that I didn't even realize I'd been missing. My chest ached as she held me and sniffled against my shoulder. She'd never been a large woman, more like a large personality, but she was frail and too light in my arms.

Aunt Ginny pulled away and wiped her eyes. "Chasen Scott Steele, aren't you a sight for sore eyes?" She gestured to someone behind her and the man took over the Bingo game. "Come on, we can visit in my room."

We walked, hand-in-hand, from the large room and down yet another hallway to a door that Ginny pushed open. She swept her hand in an inviting gesture and I entered a tiny little room with a bathroom, a hospital bed, an assistive recliner, a couch, a small table and chair, and a television.

"Why do you live here?" I blurted. "I'm sorry. I'm so glad to see you and to know we live so near each other. But why are you living *here*?"

Ginny patted my cheek. "There's the curiosity I've missed. Do you have some time? This story will take a while."

I glanced at my phone and winced. "I'm borrowing my roommate's car." I made another split-second decision. "If he can get up here to get his car, can I sleep on your couch? Do they allow you to have overnight visitors?"

Ginny waggled her brow. "Well, not the type of overnight visitors I'd *like* to have, but you sleeping over is fine."

I blushed. "Let me text Todd and tell him I can't make it back with his car."

Five minutes later, after Ginny had produced bottled water from a tiny refrigerator I hadn't noticed earlier, my phone pinged with a text filled with more expletives than anything else. I sighed.

"Need to leave?" Ginny nodded toward my phone.

I held my head in my hands. "No, but Todd is less than happy with me. He wants me out by the end of the month."

Ginny gasped. "Oh, I'm so sorry. No, you go ahead and take the car home. We can do this another time."

"No, it's not your fault. Our situation was coming to a close sooner rather than later, it's just even sooner now." I reached over the table and took her hand. "Now that I've found you," I paused at the way she smirked, "okay, now that *you've* found me, I'm not leaving until I know everything."

"Well, then, settle in my boy." Aunt Ginny took a sip of her water. "Why did you leave? Where did you go?"

I took a deep breath and gave her a sad smile. "My mom was a drug addict, alcoholic, abuser. I turned eighteen and never looked back." I shrugged and tried to swallow my anger and hurt that Aunt Ginny had never saved me.

She nodded and a tear slid down her cheek. "That's what I was afraid of. I'm so sorry I never knew. I don't know how I didn't realize it. I truly hate myself for letting you live through that. I have no excuses. Yes, I was busy traveling the world and living my best life, but there's no way I should have missed that." Ginny continued to cry silent tears. "It wasn't until you left and your mom contacted me to see if I'd seen you, that I realized something was wrong. I dropped in with no warning and found her drunk, high, and violent. The first moment I stepped into the house, I began to realize I'd made a terrible, terrible mistake." Ginny reached for a tissue as she sniffled. "Your mom went on such a rampage, saying such horrible things about you, about me, that I was quickly slapped by the reality that you'd been living with a monster and I'd had no clue."

My throat tightened and my nose burned as I blinked

rapidly. "I know now that you didn't know, but back then I wanted you to fly in, swoop me up, and save me."

Ginny sobbed and held my hand. "Why, why, why didn't you tell me? I would have taken you away from her in a heartbeat."

The tears I'd been fighting finally won. Hot wetness streamed down my face as I shook my head. "I didn't have any way to contact you. Mom never let me have a phone—at least not one of my own that I could use without her knowing. I never knew when you were coming. I didn't know how to get you away from her to tell you. And then what? I was scared to tell you and have Mom find out. What if she was worse to me? Or hurt you? Or, my biggest fear, she made you stop coming to visit?" I angrily wiped my tears. "I was a kid, I didn't have resources, I didn't have a way out."

"Did the school ever suspect or call DCS on her?" Ginny wrinkled her brow.

"No, she never left marks that could be seen. And she was more verbally abusive than physically." I leaned the side of my head against my hand. "I adored school. I was safe, warm, fed, and the teachers and most of the kids liked me. I didn't cause trouble, never told anyone about Mom, and flew under the radar for the most part. As a little kid, I figured Mom was better than being taken away. As a teen, I knew I was just biding my time. My eighteenth birthday became my goal and I worked my ass off to be sure I graduated and stayed out of trouble so I could leave. The day of my birthday, I got up, packed up everything that was *mine*—and that was very little—left anything and everything she could have used to track me. Credit card she sent me to the store with, the junk phone she only let me have once I started driving her car so she could call or text to have me get cigarettes—left it all. I didn't even take her car, left it sitting right where it was and hiked my ass to the nearest Army recruiting office and enlisted."

Ginny wept as I told my story. She squeezed my hand. "I'm so very sorry, child. My selfishness and preoccupation with traveling hurt you more than I will probably ever understand and I will never forgive myself."

"It's in the past and can't be changed now. The Army was good to me. We have each other now and I'd rather focus on the future than dwell on the nastiness of the past." I meant the words I said, even though my heart hurt as I relived the hell that had been my childhood and teen years.

"Tell me about your time in the Army. You're no longer enlisted?"

"I spent eight years serving. I was deployed about half of that time in the States and about half in South Korea." I took a sip of water.

"Oh dear, was Korea dangerous?"

"No, not South Korea. We were there as a show of force to keep North Korea under control. Well, as under control as you can keep a country like that." I had enjoyed my time in Korea and had learned a lot from their culture. I had been looking forward to another deployment to South Korea or even Germany before I fucked it up.

"Why did you leave?" Ginny cocked her head. "From the way you talk about it, you seem to have really enjoyed your time of service. Thank you, by the way, for your service. It's appreciated more than you know."

It never stopped being weird to have a person thank

me for doing something I enjoyed, but I nodded graciously. "Army was having a mandatory fun day on base, wanted to increase morale. My squad was playing a very hyped-up game of basketball against another squad. Stakes were high." I smiled wryly remembering how pumped up we'd been to dominate that stupid game. "I went up for a rebound, came down wrong just as another guy fell into me, tore my ACL. Grade two injury. I barely avoided surgery, but even after months of healing and physical therapy, the base docs determined I was medically unable to serve. Discharged. Just about two years ago."

Ginny's face held so much guilt and compassion, I felt bad for telling her my story. "I'm so very sorry you were injured like that. There's no way you can ever go back?"

I shook my head. "Nah, I'm out for good."

"Does your knee still cause you pain?"

"Sometimes. As long as I don't get too physical on it, I'm okay. No football for me, no full-on basketball games. Stairs can hurt sometimes if it's feeling stiff. Honestly, I just can't do sports or more than a few squats. Other than that, I'm okay and can do pretty much anything I need to." Almost as if my damn knee knew it was being talked about, it throbbed a bit before I shifted to a different position.

"And what do you do now?"

"Well, the Army was supposed to be my career. Planned to retire from the service. That plan got shot all to hell and I've been struggling to find a stable job since then."

"Oh dear, that's terrible. What type of work are you

looking for?" Ginny grabbed a notepad. "I have lots of friends and connections."

I smiled. "I'm sure you do." Ginny having connections didn't surprise me at all. "Honestly, I can't do jobs with a lot of climbing or squatting, but other than that, I'm open to almost anything."

"Where do you live? Where are you looking?"

"Well, I live far south of town, but now that I'm without a car and looking for a new place, I'm trying to find something in Indy." I startled as my phone buzzed on the table. Todd. I grimaced. "Todd is here to get the keys. I'll be right back."

"Nonsense, I'll have one of the orderlies deliver the keys. You don't need to interact with someone who is kicking you out." Ginny held her hand out. "Unless you *want* to go talk to Todd?"

I handed over the key. "Actually, no. He's in a beat-up black van. Red-head is probably driving. Todd is likely standing outside the van vaping. He's got long blond hair, kinda stringy, and he probably has smeared black eyeliner."

"Sounds like an interesting character." Ginny stood. "I'll be right back. Text Todd to let him know an orderly dressed in navy blue scrubs will be bringing the key."

I took a moment to use the restroom before Ginny returned. While it was amazing to be back with my aunt, I was feeling a little drained from rehashing the past. And I had a bad feeling that I was going to feel worse before I felt better. Ginny had told me nothing of the past ten years. I wondered what she needed to share with me.

## 4

---

## XANDER

I WOKE from a dream about that damn nameless stranger feeding the fucking ducks. We didn't even speak in the dream, but he was there with those stupid ducks and I woke because I watched him walk away without getting his name.

Checking the time and groaning to see I'd only been asleep about two hours, I rolled from the bed and pulled on a pair of sweats along with a tank. I was restless and irritated, might as well check the shop and work out a bit. Probably the worst thing I could do for sleeping, but maybe it would ease my frustration.

Once downstairs, I swept again. Cleaned some windows and mirrors, cleaned the public and private restrooms, and restocked paper towels. When the shop was free of absolutely anything I could possibly clean, with the exception of maybe clearing it out and waxing the floor, I went to the little weight room.

Turning on the radio that only got a local pop station, I set to work on pull-ups. I was about twenty minutes in and focusing on biceps and triceps with the dumb bells when a voice behind me nearly gave me a heart attack.

"You're here late," Bay stated blandly, but I heard the question in his voice.

Putting down the weights, I held a hand on my chest. "Damn, man. You almost killed me." I grabbed a towel and wiped my face. "Yeah, couldn't sleep. Cleaned a bit and thought maybe some weights would help."

"What did you eat for dinner? Isn't it like garbanzo beans or something that supposedly give you nightmares?" Bay hopped up and gripped the chin-up bar before doing ten in rapid succession.

"Damn, man. I hope I'm as fit as you when I'm your age." I whistled.

Bay dropped and punched me. "I'm not *that* old."

I laughed. "Nah, I don't think it was anything I ate. Bode always has good food at The Lizard. And it wasn't a nightmare."

"Man, you're gonna turn into bar food. You should come eat with Kyson and the kids and me." Bay smiled. "Well, Cori isn't eating much besides milk and pureed foods these days, maybe some soft fruits and veggies here and there, but the invite stands."

"Thanks. Don't want to intrude." I tossed the towel over my shoulder. I'd wash it before returning it to the weight room.

"Kids would love it. And by kids, I mean Kyson and Arlo." Bay chuckled. "So, what was it about?"

"Huh?" I followed him to the dimly lit shop.

Bay grabbed two waters and tossed one to me. "The not-a-nightmare?"

"Oh, uh. Nothing." I took a drink of the water.

"Nothing? Weird, *nothing* doesn't usually make a person stutter and blush." He winked.

"Really, it's nothing. Saw a guy feeding ducks at the park today. We chatted for about ten minutes and then I left. I think I'm irritated with myself for not getting his name—maybe because he's looking for a job and I can't tell him about any openings because I was dumb and didn't get his info—but other than that, it's nothing." I took another drink and tried to sneak in a subject change. "Can I ask about your kids?"

Bay smirked, but took the bait and nodded.

"Arlo is eight? And Cori is almost one?"

"Yep, I can't believe he's been with me for over four years now. And Cori was so tiny when we got her, and now she's like a little person who is into everything and likely walking any time now. It's crazy." Bay's eyes lit up like they did anytime he spoke of his family.

"Can I ask how you came to be their parents?"

Bay got a faraway look in his eyes. "Arlo was my sister's son. She left him to me when she died. Kyson officially adopted him a few years ago." Bay finished the last bit of his water. "Cori was through a private adoption. We believe her mother was very young, but other than that, we have no details beyond her health background. The mother and her family didn't want anything to do with knowing us or keeping in contact with Cori. She's named after my sister. Well, sort of. My sister was Coriander, but I'd never do that to a kid, so we went with Cori."

"Coriander? Wow, that's unique." I cocked my head. "Well, I guess Bay is pretty unique too."

He chuckled. "I'll let you in on a secret. My sister's full

name was Coriander Clove and my full name is Caraway Bay. My mom was a hippie and decided on spice names for us."

"Yeah, I can see why you went with Bay and Cori," I teased. "It's really nice that you could give those kids a good home. Like Bode and Sage are doing with Oliver and Rosie. I hate to see any kids in the foster system." I tossed my water bottle with a little more force than needed.

"I remember you telling me you have not-so-great experience with foster care." Bay eyed the trashcan where I'd thrown the bottle.

"Yeah, definitely not-so-great. So, I love seeing kids get good homes and prove that not all foster parents are assholes."

Bay nodded. "Bode and Sage are really good with Oliver and Rosie. I hope it works out that they can adopt Rosie like they did with Oliver. That kid has blossomed since living with them." Bay checked the time. "You going to stay down here?"

"Yeah, gonna work on my bike for a bit. Maybe a shower will help me sleep."

"Want me to make you some warm milk?" Bay teased.

"No, thanks, Caraway. I'm good."

Bay narrowed his eyes. "Don't use that information for evil," he warned.

We said goodbye and I settled in to mess with my bike for an hour or so. I needed to get some sleep, but I was wide awake. And I couldn't get that damn duck guy out my head.

## 5

## CHASE

"OKAY, WHERE WERE WE?" Ginny asked as she came back through the door. "We can chat for a while, go to the cafeteria for dinner, and spend the rest of the evening chatting."

I smiled. "Can't believe what a day this has been. Came into town to look for a job and found my long lost, favorite aunt." I shook my head. "I missed you so much, but I don't think I realized until today just how much."

"First, I wasn't lost." Ginny swatted at my arm. "Second, I'm your only aunt so don't try to butter me up with that *favorite* crap."

I laughed. "Maybe I have an aunt on my father's side. Never know."

"Well, while that's true, we both know your mother had no idea who your father even was, so I doubt you've suddenly come across another aunt vying for the *favorite* spot."

"Okay, true." I glanced toward the tiny living room. "Would you be more comfortable in your chair?"

Ginny huffed, but nodded and made her way to the recliner. "Now, don't laugh at an old gal lowering herself into one of these." She gripped the arms and began to sit.

"Isn't it one of those that lifts and lowers?"

"Yeah, but I like to save my pride a bit. I only use it to help me get up. I've not lost the ability to sit down." She grimaced as she finally settled in. "Not yet."

"So, Mom looked for me after I left?"

Ginny pursed her lips and nodded.

"Like looked for *me* or looked for her errand boy and emotional punching bag?" I knew the answer even before my aunt gave me a sorrowful glance.

"Well, I think you'd been gone a couple months before she contacted me. Once I realized she was an addict and likely had been abusive to you, I vowed to never tell her where you were even if I ever actually found you." Ginny rocked in her chair a bit. "I put out feelers with all my airline contacts, neighbors of your mom who knew you and might hear from you, local colleges, and hospitals. I had everyone I could think of keeping an eye out for you or your name. Like I said, I have a lot of connections. But not a single person ever came through for me. I don't know why I never thought of the military. Maybe because I didn't really have contacts there and had never heard you even mention wanting to enlist."

"I had no plans of joining the military until I was a teenager and a recruiter came to school. From that point on, I kept the plan a complete secret. Barely even allowed myself to *think* about it when I was at home for fear Mom would figure it out." I grabbed a blanket from the back of the couch and took it to Ginny before sitting down and spreading a second blanket over my lap. "I went to the library and did research. Set up a separate email for any military correspondence with recruiters. Read materials only at the library because I was scared if Mom saw a magazine she'd have an inkling of my whereabouts after I left."

"I think you give that poor excuse for a mother more credit than she deserves, but I can understand your thinking." Ginny tucked the afghan around her legs. "After you left, your mom got even worse than she'd been before. Smoked like a damn chimney, took every pill she could get her hands on, drank morning, noon, and night." She paused.

"Go on."

"Well, about two years or so after you left, your mom got pregnant. She swore up and down she didn't remember having sex with anyone—which she probably *didn't*—but she was determined to have the baby. It was like she wanted to prove something with the baby."

My heart nearly stopped. A baby? Oh my God, my mom had no business having *me* let alone another child. "What happened?" I assumed the very worst at all times if my mom was involved.

"I moved in and kept her mostly sober and clean the entire pregnancy. I thought one of us was going to end up dead, but we survived. She never once stopped smoking. As much as I wanted her to be completely healthy for the baby, I figured keeping her from drinking and taking drugs was better than nothing. She still snuck a few things from time to time, but I usually sniffed it out pretty quickly and destroyed any alcohol, pills, pot, anything."

I rubbed a hand over my chest, my heart hurt. "Did the baby die?"

Ginny's eyes snapped to mine. "What? Heavens no, child. I contacted social services and told them of my sister's drinking and drugs. I recorded and reported each time Kathryn had so much as a sip of wine or anything stronger than a Tylenol. I took pictures of all the alcohol and drug bottles I threw out when I first moved in and every time I found something she'd snuck in."

"That was really smart. She shouldn't have any chance to hurt another child."

"Social services began doing drop-ins and Kathryn went tits-up as you can imagine. Freaked out, verbally abusive, threw things at one of the ladies once." Ginny's eyes got a far-away look. "They determined that there was enough evidence against her that the baby would only go home if I was in the home and a case would be opened in order to track Kathryn's drinking and drug use."

"So, she got to keep the baby?" I knew the system was messed up, but I hated thinking of a sibling growing up with my mother.

"Turns out, the day she went into labor, your mom had somehow found a way to drink nearly a bottle of wine and pop several pain killers. She swore it was the only way she'd get through the pain. Because of the case and my insistence—maybe even as standard procedure, I'm not sure—they did bloodwork at the hospital, found her under the influence, and assigned me as temporary guardian."

My eyes grew wide. "You have the baby?" I quickly did some math. "Well, not a *baby* now. What happened?"

"We should go get dinner."

"No! You can't leave me hanging like that. What happened?"

Ginny used the remote to stand from the chair. "We'll talk as we walk and eat."

Ten minutes later, I was nearly jumping out of my skin with worry and wonder, and Ginny had prepped herself for dinner. We headed toward the cafeteria.

"After social services, the hospital, and I all spoke with your mom, she fairly easily signed away her rights." Ginny hooked her arm in the crook of my elbow. "It almost seemed unfair. We hit her hard when she was at her weakest, but I couldn't risk her being able to hurt that baby girl the way she hurt you."

"A girl? I have a sister?" The words caught in my throat.

"Little girl was born with sass and spunk enough for all three of us and then some. She and I moved into a quaint little apartment and I became a mom. Never planned to be a parent. I was likely much too old, but I was all she had, so I did the best I could."

I patted her hand as we reached the cafeteria. "You were an amazing aunt, I know you're an amazing mom."

"Your mom visited from time to time. Mostly in between bouts of using and going to treatment. She swore over and over that she'd get clean and be a good mom. Never happened." Ginny sat down and reached for a small cardboard menu.

I grunted in disgust. "Doesn't surprise me."

"Pick whatever you want. You get a main dish, a side, a vegetable, a bread, and a dessert." Ginny indicated the menu and I was, once again, hit with a punch to the gut that there was a lot more to the story. Aunt Ginny wasn't old enough to be living in assisted living.

"Wow, that's a lot of food." I perused the menu. "I'll get what you're getting."

We quickly placed our orders with one of the workers. Ginny opted for chicken and noodles, mashed potatoes, green beans, rolls, and bread pudding.

"Well, when your sister was around three, Kathryn overdosed." Ginny placed her hand on mine.

I nodded. I'd always assumed my mom would die from overdose or something similar.

"The rest of the story can wait until after dinner," Ginny whispered as our plates were brought out. "Let's eat."

I wanted to scream, but it seemed important to Ginny that we enjoy our meal, so I took a deep breath. When Ginny bowed her head for a silent grace, I followed suit out of respect.

Thirty minutes later, our food was gone and table cleared.

"Do you want coffee here or in my room?"

I raised my brows. "You make coffee as good as you used to make chocolate milk?"

Ginny laughed. "Of course."

* * *

I sipped at the steamy mug of creamy, sweet coffee as Ginny changed into her pajamas. Glancing down at the navy scrubs she'd procured for me, I smiled and recalled the sleepovers we used to have.

"Ah, that's better." Ginny returned from the bathroom and sat across from me at the tiny table. "I always love changing into more comfortable clothes. Now, I suppose you have questions."

"I do. I want to know everything." I held the mug and enjoyed the warmth that seeped into my body.

"Well, as you can tell, I don't have your sister with me any longer." Ginny's face fell and she appeared near tears. "Aside from my failure with you as a child, not being able to take care of her is my biggest regret."

"What happened?" I leaned forward on the table.

"About a year ago, I finally went to the doctor for symptoms I'd been having for several years. I'd had a feeling something was wrong even before the baby, but I was of the mind that I would simply live my life to the fullest and whatever happened would just happen. But once I became a mother, I realized I needed to be around for her as long as possible. By the time I saw the doctor, anything treatable had long since spread." Ginny lifted sparkly eyes from her mug. "I have cancer. They believe it started as breast cancer, but it's now in my lungs with several other areas also affected. I realized very quickly that it wasn't safe or realistic for me to continue caring for a child. Since social services had been involved from the very beginning, they were a huge help. They stepped in, found a placement home, and made the transition as smooth as possible. I moved in here pretty quickly; luckily, I have great benefits from my years with the airline. I'm not a candidate for chemotherapy—not that I would have gone that route. The cancer is too progressed to spend my last few months sick from chemo. I get a lot of physical therapy, breathing treatments, and homeopathic treatments, but anything else they do for me is just pain management." She smiled sadly. "If I ever seem high as a kite, it's probably the pain meds."

My heart constricted. "Months?" I'd just gotten her back.

"Well, the doctors say that the cancer is a very slow spreading one, but because it's been untreated for so long, it will just continue to spread and cause damage. But I'm as healthy as a cancer patient can be expected to be. And because I'm not doing chemo or radiation, I can go out and be as active as I feel up to being." She patted my hand. "I'm not going anywhere just yet. *Months* can mean a year or two."

"So, you still see the baby?" I frowned. "I keep saying baby when I *know* she's not that anymore." I sucked in a breath. "I don't even know what her name is."

"Oh dear, how silly of me. Her name is Rosie."

My heart swelled with an emotion I wasn't familiar with. I had a *sister*.

Rosie.

I swallowed a lump in my throat.

"I see her often. At least once a week or more. Her foster parents are amazing. I told them about you and that I was looking for you. They are open to meeting you if you're interested in meeting them and Rosie." Ginny yawned as she spoke. "Sorry, the day is catching up with me."

I wanted to meet Rosie right then and there, but it was getting late and I knew Ginny needed to rest. "Are you sure it's okay for me to stay? I'd love to meet Rosie." I frowned. "At least, I think I want to meet her. Do you think the foster parents will let me be a part of her life?" The poor girl had been born to a shitty mother, raised by a wonderful woman, then taken away because of cancer, and now thrown into a foster home. I wanted to know my sister—holy hell, I had a *sister*—but I didn't want to interrupt her life even more.

"We can go meet them tomorrow and make plans from there." Ginny stood and took my mug along with hers to the sink. "But for now, we sleep."

Ginny spent the next few minutes in the restroom. When she came out, she held up a new toothbrush. "Unused and just for you. Do you think you need more blankets or will those two be enough?"

I took the toothbrush. "Thank you. Two is fine. I've slept in much worse conditions."

Ginny frowned.

"And I didn't even have it bad. Don't worry about me. I'll be fine."

Ginny wrapped her arms around me and pulled me into a tight hug. "I'm so glad I was able to find you. Selfishly, I wanted to see you again before I die. But I also wanted to bring you and Rosie together. It's important for siblings to have each other to lean on."

"I'm not exactly sure *how* you found me, but I don't even care. I'm just glad to be here, seeing you and finding out I have a sister." I hugged her back.

Ginny just smiled and winked. "I'll never tell. But like I said, I have connections."

# 6

## CHASE

THE NEXT DAY, Ginny and I left Rose Gardens in her car.

"You can drive," she'd said as she tossed me the keys. "They let me keep the car here, and I'm not prohibited from driving—as long as I'm not taking pain medication—but I don't exactly like it. I always loved flying more than driving." Ginny settled into the passenger seat and gave me directions to a bar on Massachusetts Avenue.

"A bar?" I raised my brow.

"Well, it's a bar, but also has food. It's called The Salty Lizard. Rosie's foster parents own it and they live above it." Ginny pointed to where I was supposed to turn.

"My little sister lives above a bar?" I frowned.

"Hush, Bode and Sage are amazing with her. They adopted their son, Oliver, after fostering him, and he's doing fabulously now that he's with them. Rosie didn't really have any huge behavioral or social issues. She's super bright and is just such a great kid." Ginny gestured to a parking spot.

I pulled in and shut off the car. "Bode and Sage?"

"Her foster parents. Fathers. She adores them."

I blinked. "Fathers?"

Ginny scowled. "Yes, Rosie has two devoted, caring, generous fathers. Is that a problem?"

"No, not at all. I guess I was just picturing a mother and father." I shrugged inwardly. Two men raising my sister wasn't a problem for me, I just had to change the image I'd formed in my head. "Not like having Mom as her mother was a great situation. If two guys are treating her right and making sure she's safe and happy, I'm all for it."

For a brief moment, as I climbed from the car and joined Ginny on the sidewalk, I pictured the dark haired, dark eyed, tattooed man from the park. Did he have a wife? A partner? Kids? I huffed and shook my head. There was no reason to still be thinking about him. It was ridiculous. What did it matter? I pushed the thoughts away.

I glanced up at the bright, multicolored image of a lizard. The Salty Lizard. Well, if my sister was safe and happy, who was I to judge?

We entered through the door and I immediately felt a sense of welcoming and belonging. Two things I'd never really felt in my twenty-eight years. I belonged *to* the Army, but not really *with* them. I was welcome in the Army, but only if I was there to do my job. This place had a vibe about it that made me feel like just being me, just being here, was enough.

"That's Sage behind the bar. I imagine Bode will be out soon enough." Ginny waved toward the bar as she whispered.

Sage smiled and waved before moving toward a door

and hollering, "Bo-dee! We have guests."

I chuckled as Sage sing-songed his husband's name.

"People mispronounce Bode's name often from what I can gather. It's spelled B-o-d-e, but rhymes with Jodie —I believe his given name is *Boden*, but *Bode* fits much better. Sage likes to tease him; those two are so in love. It's beautiful, but also a little sickening." Ginny elbowed me gently as she walked to a table in the back of the bar. "This is where I usually sit when I come in."

Sage came over, followed by a dark-haired man smiling broadly.

"Ginny, we've missed you." Sage kissed my aunt's cheek. "How are you feeling?"

"Today's a good day for sure." Ginny patted Sage's cheek before being swept up in a hug by Bode.

He kissed her cheek before turning to me. "You must be Chase?"

I nodded and smiled. "Hi, nice to meet you."

We shook hands and Sage joined in the introductions. "I'm Sage. I'm so thrilled Ginny found you. She's been so hopeful."

"I'm thrilled to be found." I glanced around somewhat anxiously.

As if reading my mind, Sage patted my shoulder. "Rosie and our son, Oliver, will be along shortly. They're with Benji and Rhys for a playdate."

"Benji is my twin, Rhys is his husband. They own The Silver and Gold Creative art studio. The kids love to go play with their dogs." Bode pulled out a chair and gestured for Ginny to sit. "Let's get some food in you. What do you feel like today?" Bode asked.

"I'd love a Coke and one of those little pizzas. Just cheese."

Bode handed me a menu. "Take a look and I'll grab drinks. What'll you have?"

"Coke sounds good. Thanks."

Bode headed to get the drinks and Sage sat down with us.

"Wow, I can't believe how much Rosie looks like you." He studied me with a grin. "The hair color and eyes are exact."

"Same nose, too." Ginny smiled and dashed at a tear with her napkin.

"We thought we could all chat for a bit before bringing Rosie in. We'd love to get to know you. Ginny speaks very highly." Sage slid my Coke across the table as Bode sat down the four glasses.

"Well, hopefully I haven't changed too much in the last ten years." I took a sip.

"Nonsense, you're the same kind, caring, lovable kid as you were back then." Ginny winked. "Plus, I had someone do some digging. I know you have a virtually spotless past."

My jaw dropped before I laughed. "Your connections?"

She nodded and pretended to be very serious. "I couldn't have some hooligan sleeping over at Rose Gardens."

"What can I get for you?" Bode asked.

"I'm guessing this is one of those places where there's no bad food, but the cheeseburger and fries sounds great." I put the menu back in its spot. "Ketchup and pickles, please."

"Fry sauce?" Bode cocked a brow.

"Fry sauce? What's that? Like ranch?" I frowned.

"Oh, try it. I didn't know what it was, but it's tasty for sure," Ginny encouraged.

"Fry sauce it is then." I shrugged. I glanced around the bar as Bode headed toward the kitchen. "Do you guys need to work? I hate to take up your time."

"Nah, during the first few months of this place, we would have been struggling to keep our heads above water, but we're solid and stable these days. We've got the kitchen, bar, and floor covered so we can visit." Sage took a sip. "I'm guessing you have questions?"

"Ginny told me a lot. Why Rosie is with you, how great your son is doing, that kind of stuff." I fiddled with the edge of my napkin.

Bode joined us. "Okay, what can we answer for you?"

"Maybe just tell me about Rosie?" My eyes stung slightly as I spoke. "I never in a million years would have imagined having a sister. I don't even know how to process all of the information I've taken in since yesterday."

For the next hour, amidst our food being delivered and me trying not to groan over one of the best burgers I'd ever eaten, Ginny, Sage, and Bode regaled me with stories of Rosie. Her first steps, first word, favorite foods, favorite stuffed animal—a green frog head with a blanket body which sounded totally freaky—and funny things she'd said and done over the past seven years.

Then, as Ginny peppered in stories of me as a baby and child, Sage and Bode took turns asking me about my time in the Army and my plans for the present and future.

"Well, I'm on the hunt for a job. My position in the Army didn't really prepare me for any specific trade or career in the civilian world. I plan to go to school, but food and rent have to come first, so that means I need a stable job." I wiped my mouth and glanced around the table. "I promise I'm a hard worker. I didn't get fired from previous jobs or anything like that. Downsizing happened to one, one switched to remote work which I wasn't set up for, and one I just happened to be the last hired so first fired—or *let go* in my case."

Sage glanced at Bode and waggled his brows.

Bode frowned. "We'll keep an eye out for positions. We know a lot of business owners."

"Where do you live?" Sage asked as he munched a fry dipped in what turned out to be an unbelievably delicious fry sauce.

"Well, I was living south of town, but my rental situation with my roommate is now over. I need to find something affordable in the next couple weeks. I'm looking in the city so I can be closer to jobs and school." I sighed and took another bite of the burger. "I swear I'm not really as much of a loser as it sounds like I am."

Bode scowled. "Man, I don't know what you're talking about. You served our country for eight years. You didn't plan to mess up your knee. I hate that so many talented veterans aren't given more opportunity for stable employment. No one here thinks you're a loser, that's for damn sure."

Sage nodded and Ginny patted my hand.

When our food was cleared away, Sage glanced at his phone. "Rhys and Benji are bringing the kids."

Bode cleared his throat. "We'd like to introduce Rosie to you slowly. Let her spend some time with Ginny, then meet you? You okay with that?"

I nodded, my throat thick with emotion.

About five minutes later, a little boy burst through the front door with a tiny blonde girl hot on his heels. They screeched to a halt when they saw the four of us.

"Mama!" Rosie ran toward Ginny and threw herself in my aunt's arms.

"Hey, sweet girl. Look at how big you're getting. How's school?" Ginny kissed Rosie's cheek and stroked her hair with a bright glint in her eyes.

My heart clenched to think of how hard it was for Ginny to know she wasn't going to watch Rosie grow up.

Rosie bared her teeth and pointed to a gaping hole. "Look! I lost another tooth. It fell out at school and I swallowed it. Oliver says I'll poop it out! But Daddy and Papa said I can still gets some money for it."

Ginny made a big fuss over the lost tooth while Sage and Bode spoke to the two men who had followed the kids into The Salty Lizard. Sage gestured to me and I stood quickly to join them.

"This is Chase Steele. Ginny's nephew and Rosie's brother," Sage spoke quietly. "Chase, this is Benji and Rhys."

I shook their hands and marveled at how much alike Benji and Bode looked. Benji and Rhys were an incredibly attractive couple. Hell, every man I'd met in this damn town so far was gorgeous. And for some reason, the men I'd been meeting somehow had me reliving attractions I'd thought were long dead and forgotten. Apparently, I was wrong.

Benji and Rhys said goodbye to the kids and Ginny.

Sage and Bode introduced me to Oliver. Adorable kid.

And then we sat back down with Ginny and Rosie. I

found myself mesmerized by Rosie's stories and laughter. She was a tiny little thing, but she really did have the exact same color hair as me. And our ice-blue eyes were freakishly similar. I remembered my mom having light blue eyes, but they never twinkled or sparkled, only looked fiery with anger or dull with drug use.

All of a sudden, Rosie climbed down from Ginny's lap and scrambled over to stand in front of me with her hands on her hips. "You look like me," she accused.

Sage and Bode laughed.

"So much for going slow," Bode mumbled. "Rosie girl, this is Chase."

"Hi, Chase." She stuck her hand out. "You're supposed to shake my hand," she whispered.

I chuckled and took her hand. "Hi, Rosie. It's great to meet you."

"Why do you look like me?" Rosie's face puckered with confusion.

Oliver glanced between Rosie and me. "He's big and old, you're little and a kid, but you're the same too."

"Well," Sage pulled Rosie onto his lap, "Chase looks like you because he's your brother."

"My brother?" Rosie's eyes went wide. "But he's so big."

"Remember how your birthmother, Kathryn, couldn't take care of you so she let you have Mama?" Sage spoke quietly and Rosie nodded. "Well, Chase was a grown-up before you were born, but his mom is Kathryn just like you."

The fact that Rosie and I looked so similar made me wonder if Mom had hooked back up with my father all those years later.

"Did you know that my birthmother died?" Rosie asked.

"Yes, I learned of that recently." I nodded.

"I didn't know her. She was sick. But I gots Mama instead. Did you get another mama?" Rosie scrunched up her face.

"No, I only got one mama. You're very lucky to have your mama. She's a really good one." My words caught as Ginny squeezed my hand.

"And I gots two daddies." Rosie beamed around the little group at Sage and Bode.

"I *have* two dads, too," Oliver interrupted. At a year older than Rosie, he clearly wanted to make sure everyone knew he was more mature.

"You're both very lucky."

"And now I gots a brother." Rosie gave a little fist pump.

I was done. Gone. Head over heels for the toothless little mini-me.

My heart lurched. *Please, please let Sage and Bode be okay with me getting to know her and being a part of her life. And please let me be able to find a job and a place to live so I can be here for her.*

* * *

A couple of hours later, after we'd played several games with Oliver and Rosie in the office, Ginny wrapped the kids in a hug and kissed them both on top of their heads.

"Boys, I hate to be the pooper of the party, but this sick old lady needs to head home." Ginny kept Rosie pulled close to her side.

I glanced quickly between Ginny, Sage, and Bode.

"Rosie knows Mama is sick," Ginny added as she nuzzled her chin against the little girl's hair.

"Mama is sick. Not sick like my other mom. That's why I gets two daddies. Mama wants to spend time with me, but she gets tired, so I live here and Mama visits." Rosie patted Ginny's leg.

"Bode, would you be so kind as to get Chase home for me? I don't want him to have to leave just because I'm dragging." Ginny might as well have batted her lashes at the older man.

"Absolutely." Bode nodded.

"No, that's not necessary." I held up my hand and shook my head.

"Nonsense, you've just met your sister. Stay and visit. Get to know her and the guys." Ginny gave me an encouraging nod.

"Really, we'd love to have you stay for a while. Rosie already adores you and I'm sure she and Oliver would be thrilled to have a captive audience for a while this evening." Sage raised a brow in question.

"Are you okay to drive? Maybe I should drive you home." I searched Ginny's face for any sign of exhaustion.

"I've not taken any prescription medication. I'm calling it quits before I'm too tired to drive. I'll be fine. Promise."

"Ginny always has us drive her if she's not feeling up to it. You can trust her." Bode smiled softly at my aunt.

Ginny hugged Rosie and the guys before turning to me. "I expect weekly visits. At least one or two days a week. And texts. I'm so glad to have you back." She wrapped me in her arms and stood on her tiptoes to kiss my cheek.

"You couldn't keep me away," I promised.

Once Ginny had taken her leave, Sage asked if I wanted to walk to the park with the kids and him. My first thought was of the tattooed stranger. Would he be there?

I agreed to the walk while silently chastising myself. Maybe we weren't even going to the same park. What the hell was wrong with me and why could I not get that guy off my mind?

7

———

CHASE


TURNED out we did go to the same park. We fed the ducks because Rosie and Oliver adored tossing the food into the water and watching the quacking ducks scramble for pieces.

As the kids laughed and played, running back and forth from the ducks to the playground to where Sage and I sat between the two areas, we made small talk and chuckled at the kids.

"What type of work are you looking for? Anything you absolutely can't or won't do?" Sage held out his hand and took another rock Oliver wanted to take home for his collection.

Before I could answer, I found myself beaming at Rosie who thrust leaves and flowers into my hand. "Can you hold these, please? I want them for my collection, too."

"Sure thing." I gingerly arranged the handful of foliage as she ran off to play. "Honestly, I'm not against any type of work as long as it's legal. I can't do a ton of squatting or running, but I'm able to do most anything else. If the knee hurts from being on it too much, I slap on a brace and ice it later."

"You looking for a place by yourself or with roommates?"

I shrugged. "Whichever I can find. Roommates would probably be cheaper. I've lived with a lot of different types of people thanks to the Army. I can get along with pretty much anyone. I'd prefer my own room, that's about my only request."

After a pause in the conversation, I changed the subject to focus on Sage. "You work at the bar while the kids are in school?"

Sage nodded. "I moved in with Bode, Benji, and Kyson when they all lived above The Lizard and I was in school. Bode hired me on part time after a while." He smiled. "Bode and I took a while to figure things out between us, but we've been inseparable ever since." He paused for a moment and watched the kids. "I had every intention of getting a job straight after graduation, but then I got struck with the crazy idea to elope and become foster parents. I've never looked back. My main job is the kids; we usually have an additional one or two at any given time. Oliver, of course, is full time. And Rosie is full time for now."

"Are you hoping to adopt her?" I realized quickly that I very much wanted my sister to belong to Sage and Bode. I felt deep in my heart that she'd be safe and happy with them.

"We'd love to. Just have to see how things work out. Ginny has indicated she wants to see it happen before she dies." He watched the kids play, but his voice held sadness. "I hate that she lost her birthmother and now

Ginny." Sage turned toward me. "That's why I'm so glad you're here. We'd love for you to be a part of her life."

My heart caught in my chest and all I could do was nod and turn my attention to watch Oliver and Rosie on the swings. I rapidly blinked away the sting of tears.

After a moment or two, I'd collected myself enough to respond. "I'd love to be a part of Rosie's life. I'm really hoping I can land a stable job and place to stay so I can see her often." I cleared my throat. "I appreciate you and Bode allowing me a place in her little world."

"We've known Ginny long enough now to completely trust her judgment. If she vouches for you it's all good."

I chuckled. "Well, at least you know she had my records checked."

"Yeah, there *is* that, too." Sage laughed and stood. "Probably better be getting back. The dinner crowd will start soon. And I'll need to get the kids in the bath and to bed."

"Does living above a bar cause issues with their sleep?" I asked as we waited for the kids to take one last ride on the slide.

"No, not at all. We worried a bit when Oliver came to stay with us, but that kid could sleep through a marching band playing by his bed. And Rosie used a sound machine at Ginny's so we use one here. She wakes sometimes for a drink, but goes back to bed easily." Sage took each kid's hand as we headed toward the exit. "Sadly, a lot of foster kids are so angry at being taken from their home or so relieved to have a warm, safe place to stay that they don't even notice the noise."

I threw one last look toward the duck pond. No motorcycle man.

"Do they stay upstairs alone while you're working?" I didn't mean to sound accusatory, but I was curious.

"Once they are bathed and in bed, I'll run up and down the stairs and take turns with Bode checking on them. We have camera baby monitors set up in their rooms, so we can hear and see them one hundred percent of the time. It takes about five seconds from the bar to the apartment, so we feel really safe with the set up." Sage glanced at Rosie and leaned down so she could whisper something to him. He nodded and smiled. "Plus," he added, "we are checked on by social services to be sure the children are safe and well cared for."

"I didn't mean any offense," I started, but I was cut off by Rosie moving to my side and taking my hand. My breathing froze and my heart stopped.

"None taken." Sage winked and beamed down to where Rosie's tiny hand was swinging mine back and forth as we walked.

"Now we all gots a hand to hold," Rosie exclaimed as we made our way back to The Salty Lizard.

\* \* \*

Bode brought me a Coke and a laptop. "I'm going to take the kids up to get a bath. Sage is helping with food in the kitchen. Feel free to browse for jobs and apartments. He'll be out in a bit with something to eat."

"Oh, I'm good." A thought hit me. "Shit, I haven't paid for lunch." I reached for my wallet. I wasn't broke, but I really didn't need to spend money on two meals that day.

"Nope, lunch and dinner on the house. Ginny always eats for free. As Rosie's brother, you will too."

I shook my head. "I can't eat for free every time. That's not fair."

"We'll work it out. Today's food is free. Period." Bode knocked his knuckles on the table and turned to leave.

About an hour later, after I'd emailed myself about twenty somewhat promising jobs and a much smaller selection of possibly feasible apartments, Sage came out with a tray.

"Dinner is served," he said as he placed the tray on the table. "The rush has slowed a bit so we can eat and then I'll go back and help with clean-up. Or I'll take over with the kids and make Bode do clean-up." Sage winked.

"That's a lot of food." I eyed the tray. Tater-tots, a small pizza, fries and sauce, onion rings, and Brussels sprouts.

"I just took extras or things that were mess-ups. The pizza was supposed to be light sauce. The sprouts were supposed to be no salt. It's all good. Dig in." Sage trotted over to the bar and filled two glasses with soda before joining me at the table.

A few minutes into the meal and our casual chatter, I glanced up as the front door opened. A tall, dark-haired man in a black t-shirt entered and I nearly choked on a fry. The tattoos were unmistakable. It was the guy from the duck pond. I watched as he walked to the bar, took a seat, and spoke to the bar tender.

"You know him?" Sage asked, an amused look on his face.

"Not really. Met him at the duck pond yesterday." Wow, was that just yesterday? "Didn't even catch his name."

"That's Xan, he's a good guy." Sage caught the man's attention and waved him over.

My heart beat double time as I tried to remember how to speak. *Dumbass, you're saying hi to someone you've already spoken to. Sage knows him. Settle yourself. It's a conversation, means nothing.*

"Hey, I know you," the guy said. "Well, not your name, but you get the point." He stuck his hand out. "I'm Alexander. Some people call me Xander. If I like you, you can call me Xan." He winked.

My stomach fluttered. "So, can I call you Xan?" *Dear Lord, was I flirting?* I seriously had no idea what it was about this guy that had me acting completely foreign.

Xan held my hand for a second longer than necessary. "Depends. What can I call you?"

My cheeks heated. "Real name is Chasen, but I mostly go by Chase."

"Nice to meet you, Chase." He waved at the bartender and then pulled out a chair and sat at our table. "So, you love The Salty Lizard as much as I do, huh? And just how did you get mixed in with this guy?" Xan elbowed Sage and laughed.

"Just learned of both The Lizard and Sage today." I winced. "It's kinda a very long story."

"Chase is Rosie's brother," Sage offered.

Xan's eyes grew wide. "No shit? Wow. Damn, I can totally see the resemblance. It's the eyes and the hair." He glanced between Sage and me. "But, wait, you just met Sage today. So, did you not know about Rosie?"

I shook my head. "After I talked to you yesterday, I was supposed to go get more applications. But I got a text from my aunt who I hadn't seen or heard from in ten years—not by choice—and found out she lives here in Indy. Went to see her, rehashed a pretty shitty past, learned she's dying, and found out I have a seven-year-old sister." I blew out a breath. "Wow, that still sounds unbelievable."

"Truth is sometimes stranger than fiction, man." Xan popped an onion ring in his mouth after dipping it in fry sauce. "If you guys ever stop with the sauce, I may have to find somewhere new to eat."

"You eat here practically every night. You'd never survive." Sage rolled his eyes.

"Truth." Xan grinned and ate another onion ring.

"So, how do you guys know each other?" I asked. My heart sunk when I realized it was a very real possibility that Xan was a partner to someone in their group.

"Xan works for Bay at Whitfield's," Sage started.

I nodded because I knew that part.

"Bay is married to Bode's cousin, Kyson. They have Arlo and a new baby, Cori," Sage explained.

"When I started at Whitfield's, Bay told me about this place and I've pretty much eaten at least one meal a day here since then."

"I'd guess sometimes two since you usually take home leftovers." Sage poked at Xan's ribs. "It's a wonder you've not turned into a blob of grease."

"Hey! I eat the veggies you guys have." Xan scowled. "I'm healthy-ish."

"Most of the veggies we have are fried or dipped in cheese," Sage countered.

"Okay, okay, I should try to broaden my horizons and eat more nutritious food from time to time." Xan sighed. He looked at me. "You'd think he'd *want* my business.

But, oh no, he wants to kick me out and make me go eat kale and tofu."

"We love you here. I'm just saying that bar food isn't always the best for you." Sage smirked as he dipped a fry in sauce.

"But it tastes *so* good," Xan whined. His food was delivered at that moment and he breathed in deeply. "Ahhh, smell the greasy goodness."

"I hope you're going to run or lift or *something* after this. I don't want to be responsible for your heart attack." Sage shook his head.

"I'll lift. And I'm active all day at the shop." Xan took a big bite of his burger. "Maybe I'll take Bay up on the offer to eat with them one night. I bet Bay and Kyson cook healthy for the kids."

"We should actually do a big group dinner sometime. I know the kids would love to play." Sage sipped his drink. He checked his phone. "I need to head upstairs to help with the kids so Bode can come down. Chase, you want to come with me and say goodnight to Rosie?"

Half of me wanted to stay and talk to Xan. But I definitely wanted to see my sister again. So, I wiped my mouth on the napkin and finished my drink.

"Oh, okay. I'll just eat alone. I see how it is." Xan mocked offense.

"Sorry, little sister I just found out about wins every time," I joked.

"Definitely. I get it. Nice knowing your name." Xan ducked his head a bit and I swore I saw a blush on his cheeks. "Maybe see you around since we seem to have a similar circle of friends?"

"Well, I wouldn't say I have many friends, but yeah." I smiled.

Xan cocked his head and studied me for a moment before turning to Sage and saying goodbye.

As I followed Sage up the stairs to the apartment, I fought the urge to grin like a fool. I knew his name. I'd see Xan again almost for sure.

"He's cute." Sage nudged me as we stood outside the door.

My face was on fire and I said nothing.

* * *

Oliver and Rosie were fresh and clean from their baths. They each brought a book to the couch and scrambled up onto the cushions before glancing at Sage and me expectantly.

Sage gestured toward the couch. "Settle in. It's story time."

I nervously sat down and nearly melted when Rosie shifted to sit on my lap.

"I want Chase to read my book," Rosie exclaimed.

*Oh, shit*. I hadn't read a kid's book in twenty years. And now I was going to read aloud to an audience. *Fuuuck*. But I already knew I couldn't say no to my little sister.

Sage saved me by reading Oliver's book first.

Somehow, I survived reading *Chicka Chicka Boom Boom* without stumbling too much, then moved to Rosie's purple and teal unicorn and dragon room in a haze. I listened to Rosie and Sage say their goodnights, found myself being hugged and kissed on the cheek, and saying goodnight to Rosie. Before I'd left her room, I'd somehow agreed to seeing her again very soon.

I wanted to see her, but I was learning that I had little control over my decisions when Rosie was involved.

Sage sat down on the couch and pointed to the recliner. "Have a seat." He chuckled. "You look like you're in a bit of a daze."

I sat and shook my head. "It's just weird. Yesterday, I was alone. Today, I have my aunt and a *sister*. Crazy."

"You're not alone. You've also got the whole Silver crew." Sage smiled warmly and my heart soared.

Bode came in the door. "They go down okay?"

Sage nodded.

"I've got a suggestion." Bode glanced my way. "Would you be willing to spend the night? After Sage takes the kids to school in the morning, he can take you home."

"I couldn't do that, I don't want to intrude."

"If you're not comfortable with it, that's okay. But we're completely on board with you staying. We have an extra room." Bode cleared his throat. "To be completely honest, I did my own searches on your background." He gave a sheepish look to Sage. "And I *may* have asked a friend in law enforcement to see what he could find."

"Bode! You didn't, please say you didn't. You know he's not supposed to do that." Sage's eyes were comically wide.

"He didn't tell me any details, just that Chase's background is clear." Bode glanced my way. "Sorry, just had to be sure."

"I'm glad you did. I'd be worried if you invited me to stay with you and your kids without checking up on me."

I chewed on my lip. "I can stay. If you're sure it's no trouble. I'd love to take Rosie to school."

Bode grinned broadly. "Settled then. We'll see you in the morning." He pulled Sage close and kissed him. "I'll be back up in a bit."

A weird sensation fluttered in my gut. Was I offended by the kiss? Not at all. Then why did I feel strange?

*Maybe because it kinda turned you on and you're thinking about Xan?*

I shook my head to clear my mind and push away the thought.

Sage got me set up in the spare room with a phone charger, a towel, clothes, and a toothbrush. "The bathroom is yours if you want to shower. Should be plenty of toothpaste, shampoo, and soap."

"Thanks. Appreciate it."

"Holler if you need anything. See you in the morning."

After a shower, I plugged my phone into the wall, settled into bed, and took a deep breath. Growing up with my worthless mother and eight years in the Army hadn't prepared me for the unsettled, hopeful, warm feelings that filled my soul as I waited for sleep to come.

# 8

## XAN

I WAS RESTLESS AS FUCK.

*Seems to be a constant state for you lately. At least, ever since you met Chase.*

I growled and ran a hand over my face.

After Chase and Sage had gone upstairs, I ate my dinner mechanically and headed home.

Tried to watch a movie. Couldn't keep my mind on it. I flopped around on the couch, trying to get comfortable. Twenty minutes later, I focused on the film enough to realize I'd inadvertently turned on Spanish subtitles. Angry with myself, I pointed the remote at the television and punched the *Off* button. Hard.

I pulled out a book on motorcycle repair. After about ten minutes, I'd read the same page four times. I slammed the book shut.

I stomped to the kitchen and rummaged for a beer before slamming shut the refrigerator door. I thumbed through my phone and turned on some loud, angry hard rock before picking up the latest copy of *Hot Bike*. Bay had started tossing the new issue at me a week into my position at Whitfield's. *"Bring it to the shop when you finish."*

As I noisily flipped the pages, I knew I was growing more frustrated. Nothing seemed to be helping with the irritated restlessness.

Video game? *Eh, don't really feel like it.*

Sketch a new tattoo? *I do need to do that, but right now it would just be a mess.*

Write it down? *Stupid therapists with DCS were always encouraging me to write about my feelings when I was younger. The idea wasn't terrible, but I couldn't focus enough to write at that moment.*

Run? *Bingo.*

I yanked on running clothes, popped in earbuds, and locked the door behind me as I clamored down the stairs. I absolutely *hated* running, but I knew it would help me pound out the frustration.

*Maybe you could get rid of the frustration if you'd admit what's got you so worked up.* My feet slapped against the asphalt as a cool fall breeze teased with the promise of winter not too far away. Without thinking, I ran to the park where I'd first seen him.

*Chase.*

Was he what had me feeling so irritated and restless?

*Gee, you think? You've been a hot mess since you first spoke to him. Seeing him tonight and getting a name didn't ease the burn in your chest, did it? You keep trying to tell yourself you were just frustrated that you hadn't gotten his name. But now you know his name and the burn is still there, flaming higher and hotter.*

"Shut. Up." I spit the words out between gritted teeth as I started a second lap around the little park. My head was overthinking things. I knew Chase's name now. I'd see him around. I knew how to contact him if I saw anything about job openings or an apartment. He wasn't the reason for my restless frustration.

*You sure about that?*

"Fuck off." I turned up my music louder and took a couple more laps.

By the time I breathlessly returned to my apartment, I was a sweaty mess. I went to the weight room in the shop and did pull-ups until my arms were quivering noodles. I needed a shower. Then I'd settle in with a Netflix show and try to get some decent sleep.

I took the stairs two at a time and stripped out of my clothes quickly. I threw the whole pile in the washer. I'd run the washer later; my water heater didn't keep me in enough hot water for washing clothes and a simultaneous shower.

I turned the shower on and waited for the water to warm up. Once it was hot, I climbed in and sighed as the hot water sluiced over my tired, sweaty body. The run had definitely worked out some of my jittery restlessness. At least physically. My *mind* still bounced around like a million ping pong balls in a room full of cats.

When Bay gave me a job and a place to stay, introduced me to his family and friends, I didn't find myself thinking about him—or any of them—beyond just being grateful for the opportunity and grateful to have some acquaintances who would maybe become friends. And, now that that whole crew actually were friends of mine, I felt the warmth of being welcomed.

But...

It was like something was still missing. Like my life

puzzle was starting to be pieced together, but the main pieces weren't clicking yet.

Was Chase one of those main pieces? We seemed very different at first, but I wondered if maybe we were more similar than I'd originally thought. Was he looking for a place to belong as much as I was?

Were Chase and I destined to meet because we both needed a friend—a true connection—as badly as we needed our next breath?

Or was I crazy and trying to make something out of nothing?

I rinsed shampoo from my hair before soaping up and washing away the sweat from the run. Lathering my hand before replacing the soap on the ledge, I slicked my palm over my dick.

*You know a good jerk-off session would relax you and help you sleep.*

"Shut up, you're so immature and horny," I berated my stupid mind. But my dick plumped as I continued to run a soapy hand over myself.

Sex as an eager teen had been great—despite now knowing it was wrong the way the clubs basically sold me to the highest bidders. I didn't know better back then. I was just happy to get the attention and have a place to bury my dick. But, as I got older, sex had lost some of its appeal. I found women beautiful. Definitely. But I didn't try to get with every girl I met.

I gripped my cock and stroked slowly as it grew harder.

*What if you were thinking about Chase?*

My hand faltered on my dick.

No way was I jerking off to images of him.

*Then why are you picturing blonde hair and ice-blue eyes?*

My cock was fully hard and begging to be stroked hard and fast. I needed to get off, not think about Chase.

*But think of how it would feel to take his cock in your mouth. Taste him, tease him.*

I groaned and stroked harder.

*Think of how good he'd look on his knees in front of you as you fed your cock between those pale pink lips.*

"God damn it," I bit out as the image filled my head.

Never before had I given into my curiosities about gay sex. In the beginning—and even recently, before I left the clubs—it was for my own protection, but since being free and on my own, I hadn't really thought of it much. I was focused on surviving.

But now?

Now, I couldn't rid my head of the picture of Chase's strong body kneeling before me and taking my throbbing cock deep in his throat.

My release exploded from me and I shuddered as my dick pumped hot and thick onto the tile wall. I fell forward, leaning on my bent arm, and breathing as hard as if I'd just finished a run.

*Fuck.*

That could *not* happen again. Was Chase even gay? Or bi? I'd just met the man. It appeared we'd be seeing each other at least casually quite often since our circles crossed quite a bit. We were acquaintances. Hopefully friends— fuck knows I needed a friend. I did *not* need to fuck things up by lusting over the guy.

If—and only IF—Chase and I became friends and he indicated he was possibly interested in something more, only then could I entertain thoughts of being with him sexually. Period.

*Tell that to your dick.*

I ignored my mind and got out of the shower. Once dried, I climbed into bed with my laptop. A few shows and then I'd sleep.

An hour later, as much as I tried to stop thinking about Chase, I was rock hard again. I put the computer away and took my cock in my hand like a damn horny teen who just discovered masturbation.

With my eyes squinted tightly shut, I began to pump my dick. I could jack off without thoughts of anyone in particular. I'd get off and go to sleep. Not a big deal.

But as my balls drew up tight, I licked my lips and moaned as my traitorous mind pictured Chase's cock pushing between my lips. Imaginary me teased his head and dipped my tongue in his slit, took his length deep into my mouth, my nose pressing against a blond thatch of pubic hair. I cupped my balls as the me in my imagination fondled Chase's balls. My cock erupted, spilling over my fist and stomach as my vision of Chase exploded down my throat.

When I'd caught my breath, I reached for a tissue and cleaned up.

Flat on my back, arm over my forehead, I stared into the darkness for several minutes. I needed to sleep. I need to stop thinking about Chase in a sexual way. I needed him as a friend and I didn't want to make anything awkward.

*Shit.*

I was fucked.

\* \* \*

The next day, I dragged myself from bed. Part of the night, I'd slept like the dead. Part of the night, I'd tossed and turned as I'd chastised myself for the thoughts I'd kept having about Chase.

How did I even know if he and I would get along? Maybe we'd spend more than a few minutes talking and find we had absolutely nothing in common and couldn't stand each other's guts.

*Would that make you feel better when you fuck your hand and think about him?*

I growled to myself, padded to the bathroom to brush my teeth and piss, and threw on work clothes. Within five minutes, I was downstairs with a steaming mug of coffee from the workroom, and ready to throw myself into what I knew best.

Motorcycles never threw me for a loop. Never fucked up my head. Never made me question who I was.

As I grabbed my tools and settled in to diagnose and start working on a Kawasaki Ninja ZX-6R, I thought about the whole questioning who I was thing. I'd always known I found both men and women attractive. I'd never been in a situation where I could act on the same-sex attraction. Now that I *could* act on it, I found myself in a conundrum. I knew I was surrounded by supportive people. I wasn't worried about being shunned or ridiculed for coming out as bisexual.

But did I want to act on it with Chase?

Partly, yes. Partly, no.

Was it stupid to take a barely-there, fledgling friendship and introduce physical, sexual attraction to it?

Probably.

But if I didn't act on it with Chase, then who?

What if I started sleeping with or dating guys and it pushed Chase away?

Well, if me being bisexual pushed Chase away, maybe he wasn't a good candidate for a friend.

"Man, who pissed in your Wheaties?" Jorge asked.

I jerked my head up and looked at the man grinning down at me. "What?"

"You're working that bike over like you're seeking a painful revenge."

I shook my head. "Nah, my mind's just somewhere else."

"Well, you've got a visitor out front." Jorge threw his thumb over his shoulder. "Oh, and Cliff can't take a Harley coming in today, he's booked solid. He said to push it your way. You want it?"

I wiped my hands and nodded. "Definitely. Put it on my list." I pushed the thoughts of Chase to the back of my head. Sexuality wasn't something on a fixed point. I didn't need to label myself or make decisions right then. I'd see about Chase and I working out as friends first. Decisions could be made after that.

Now, who the hell would be coming to visit me?

Chase? My heart flip-flopped.

Anyone else I knew in town was close enough to Bay, they'd just walk right in the shop.

I walked out the door to the shopfront.

And froze.

"There he is. Thinking he's all grown up and doesn't need his boys." A gravelly voice poured over my skin and made the hairs on the back of my neck stand up. "Did you think we wouldn't find you?"

Ervin "Chrome" Davis.

One of the top cronies in the last club I was in. How the fuck did he find me? He was a bad motherfucker and I did *not* want anything to do with him.

I took a quick breath and forced a smile as I walked toward him. "Chrome, man, how's it going? What are you doing in town?" I hoped that last part didn't sound as anxious and pathetic to Chrome as it did in my head. Maybe my voice could have squeaked a bit more to really let him know I was freaking out.

"Just happened to be going through Indy. Always try to find the bike shops when I'm visiting a new town. You know how I like to connect with fellow crews. After you hightailed it out, I always make it a point to ask each shop if they know of an Alexander Copperfield. You've made quite the trek since you left us." Chrome took a long drag on his cigarette.

"Yeah, had to face some personal demons, ya know?" I didn't trust Chrome or anyone in his crew. His club wasn't like some of the others where there were at least a few good eggs. No, the Pit Vipers were a nasty bunch as a whole. I really needed him to leave. I tried to shake the bad feeling I had about him finding me.

It wasn't like I'd been purposely hiding, but the fact that Chrome now knew where I worked was not a good thing. My biggest fear was him or the club bringing trouble to Bay's business.

"Demons will getcha if you're not careful." Chrome glanced at the Whitfield's sign. "Looks like you found a soft landing for that pretty ass." He chuckled evilly. "Figure you have no reason to leave these digs, but know you've got a place in the Pit if you ever find yourself

wanting to crawl back. We'll only make you grovel a bit."
He laughed at his own words.

"You good out here?" Bay was suddenly at my side.

I wasn't sure if I was relieved to have him there or
upset that I'd now have to tell him about Chrome. No, I
would have told him either way. Right? Yeah, I would
have told him. Couldn't risk hiding it and having
something bad happen.

"Chrome Davis," Ervin said as he stuck out his hand.

Bay's eyes glinted with anger as he shook Chrome's
hand. "Bay Whitfield. What brings you to our fine
establishment?"

"Just in town and I always like to meet fellow business
owners and bike enthusiasts. Been missing Xander's
talents since he left us high and dry." Chrome gave a
smarmy smile.

"Your loss is our gain. I'm sure you had talent waiting
in the wings to take his place. Good mechanics aren't
jobless for long. You got a card?" Bay reached into his
wallet and produced his own business card.

Chrome's tongue darted out to wet his bottom lip and
he chuckled. "Sure do, sure do." He pulled out a card and
the two men exchanged information. "Good to meet you,
Bay. *Alexander*, a pleasure to see you again. Know that
your spot is always open." He glanced up at the
Whitfield's sign again before throwing a look through the
windows. With a weaselly smile and a wave, Chrome
walked across the street and climbed on a bike.

"Friend of yours?" Bay asked sardonically.

"Not quite. Wasn't planning on my crappy past ever
coming here. Didn't exactly try to hide, just never thought
anyone would care enough to find me." I ran a hand over

my face. "Shit, I'm sorry. I really hope that was just a coincidental visit and not something that leads to an issue."

"You did nothing wrong. You're legally employed doing legal work. Your past is your past."

"Even when the past finds the present?" I couldn't shake the bad feeling.

"You planning on going back to them?"

"No." I shook my head. But I knew how persuasive the Pit Vipers and Chrome could be. If they had a reason to find me, if they needed me for something, they'd stop at nothing to recruit my services. I wasn't strong enough to say no back then. Would I be able to turn them down now? I wanted to say yes.

God, I hoped they'd stay away from me so I didn't have to find out.

## 9

---

## CHASE

I SLOWLY CAME AWAKE in the most comfortable bed I'd ever slept in. Clearly, I was dreaming. Someone in my dream was brewing coffee and children were laughing.

My eyes flew open.

Not a dream.

I was in Sage and Bode's spare room.

Oliver and Rosie were laughing outside my door.

My *sister* was on the other side of the door.

Coffee.

I definitely needed coffee.

The last couple days came rushing over me and threatened to drown me in overwhelming thoughts and emotions.

I rolled from bed and padded to the bathroom. A quick piss, face wash, and toothbrushing found me back in the bedroom. I assumed the guys would want to wash the sheets after I slept in them, but I made the bed anyway. I wasn't the type to leave a bed unmade, especially as someone's guest.

As I quietly opened the door, I was overcome with nervous anticipation. Sage and Bode were nice, they invited me to stay, there was no reason to feel like I was intruding or needed to sneak around.

Yet, I found myself just outside of the kitchen eavesdropping on Sage and Bode. I hadn't *meant* to slink in the shadows and listen to their conversation, I just wasn't exactly sure where I wanted to be and their words caught my attention. Before I knew what was happening, I was spying like a damn spying spier.

"Think about it. It's like fate. Remember when you didn't want me to move in here? You did everything you could to convince the guys to pick someone else. But you ended up with me and it turned out to be fabulous." Sage's words were low and persuasive. "Ginny finds her long-lost nephew, he discovers his aunt and a sister he never knew, *and* it looked very much like he and Xan are totally hitting it off."

"Babe, he's a complete stranger." Bode's words were gruff.

"Ginny had his records checked. *You* checked his records—even had Mark check them which I'm still not okay with. We could run a complete check for employment." Sage paused and I heard the soft noises of a gentle kiss.

Bode groaned.

I was a total perv hiding in the shadows and getting turned on knowing Sage and Bode were kissing.

"We need an employee. We have an extra room." Sage was laying it on thick. "We could help bring two siblings together and maybe even strike a love connection."

Bode began to speak, but I missed what he said

because I nearly shit myself as Rosie gripped my hand and basically screamed, "Whatcha doin? Why you hidin?"

Sage and Bode stuck their heads out of the kitchen and I prayed to melt into a puddle right there. Rosie shrugged when she realized it wasn't a game and went back to playing with Oliver.

"I'm sorry, I didn't mean to listen in." My words poured from me like the pathetic excuse they were. "Really, I came for coffee, heard Sage and didn't want to interrupt. By the time I realized you were talking about me, it was too late and I was frozen." I ran a hand over my face, my cheeks on fire. "Shit, I'm so sorry."

"Don't sweat it," Sage assured and waved a dismissive hand in the air. "Coffee?"

Since I wasn't lucky enough to die on the spot, I nodded and entered the kitchen. "Yes, please."

"Well, what would you think?" Bode leaned against the counter.

"About?" I stammered.

Sage beamed at Bode. It was clear Sage had won. Something told me Sage often won when it came to winning over Bode.

"Sage is right. We *do* need an employee at The Lizard. We lost quite a few people to college graduation or busy school schedules." Bode shrugged. "We planned on inviting you to be around as much as possible to build a relationship with Rosie. If you'd be willing to have a complete background check, the position and room are yours."

I stared at him for years. Decades even.

"What's wrong with him? Did I break him?" Bode scowled and spoke out of the corner of his mouth to Sage.

Sage chuckled and moved closer to me. He pushed my jaw up. "Close your mouth, sweetie." He stepped between me and Bode. "Chase, would you like a job at The Salty Lizard? It's not glamorous or exciting." He frowned. "Actually, it can be kinda exciting sometimes. And it's always fun. Great people." He dipped his head to catch my eyes. "Chase? Job? You want it?"

I nodded and tried to work my sandpapery thick tongue. "Yes, yes, of course, I want it." I tried to breathe, but my lungs seemed to be faltering.

"We have a room here. You'd pay rent, but it's a decent price. We'd set some ground rules. You'd have to be okay living with kids." Sage spoke slowly as if trying to explain quantum physics to me. "Would you like the room?"

"I, um, I just can't. I mean, *yes*, of course I'd want the room, but I can't ask you guys to give me a job, give me a room, *and* let me hang with my sister. It's too much." I moved to the right and leaned against the sink.

"Want to talk about the rent and salary? Make a decision from there?" Sage patted my arm.

I nodded mutely.

Sage went to check on the kids and set them up with crayons and coloring books along with Kidz Bop on a tablet.

Bode and I sat at the dining room table.

Sage joined us. "Okay, let's get into specifics."

Bode pulled a notebook from a drawer next to the table. Over the next twenty minutes, he detailed the hourly salary, how tips worked, the rent, and what the position at the bar would entail.

I swallowed thickly and shook my head. "I don't even know how this is happening."

"If you move in with us, we will expect you to take responsibility with chores and whatnot. You can get groceries on your own, or go with us when we do our weekly trip. Utilities are figured into the rent. Internet, cable, WiFi is through The Lizard, but it's good and you can use it." Bode made some more notes. "If you want the job and the room, we'll get all the official paperwork set up."

"We can discuss more specifics, but house rules would include remembering there are kids around." Sage drew circles on the table with a single finger. "We don't care if you bring someone home, but keep it discreet. No smoking or drugs. We drink from time to time, but we're not getting plastered and prefer you don't either. At least not in front of the kids." He paused. "Maybe help with the kids from time to time. Obviously, they are our responsibility, but we'd maybe ask for favors here and there."

"She's my sister, it's not like she's some random kid a stranger is asking me to help with."

Sage and Bode exchanged looks and then we all laughed as I realized what I'd said. "Okay, we started as strangers, but you know what I mean."

"Thoughts?" Bode raised an eyebrow.

"I mean, I can't possibly turn down a job, a room, and a chance to get to know my sister." I took a deep breath. "I'm in."

"Yes," Sage hissed. "You're going to love the Silver crew, and I know you're already getting to know Xan."

Bode's eyes went wide. "You know Xan?"

My face heated. "Met him the day Ginny found me.

Talked by the duck pond. Didn't even get his name. Sage introduced me to him yesterday at The Lizard."

Bode laughed. "Sounds like Xan. He's one of our most loyal customers since moving here. He's a great guy, you couldn't do much better."

*Shit*. What did he mean by that? Could they tell I found Xan attractive? Did they think I was gay? Was that going to be a problem?

"Oh, um, I'm not gay. Is that okay?" The words spilled from my mouth before I could control them.

Bode chuckled and Sage smiled.

"We don't discriminate. Gay, bi, trans, het, cis, we judge only on the way you treat people." Sage took my hand. "But are you *sure* you're not gay? Maybe just a bit? Because I've got to say, the way you watched Xan yesterday had me getting all hot and bothered."

"Lord, Sage, you're going to kill him," Bode teased.

My cheeks were on fire. "I mean, I've only ever been with girls. Not many. But I've found guys attractive. So, bi? Maybe?" I ran a hand over my face. "Shit, I don't know."

"But you like Xan?" Sage prodded.

"I think he's hot. We've spoken all of ten minutes. Can't say I *like* him." I shrugged.

"Good enough. We'll let you be. No matter what, you're welcome here as long as you're kind and good. That's all we ask." Bode rapped his knuckles on the table.

"We need to get the kids to school." Sage pushed back from the table with such force that I was immediately on alert that our discussion had likely put the family completely off schedule.

"I'm sorry, are they late?" I winced.

"Not at all. Today is a late arrival day. The teachers go in at the regular time and have meetings. The kids come at lunch. But, lunch starts at ten-thirty for some, so we should get going." Sage hollered to the kids and they came running to grab their lunchboxes.

Rosie took my hand. "I want to show you my school and my class and my cubby and my desk," she prattled on and on as we descended the stairs.

And I wondered if my heart would ever stop feeling so warm and full.

# 10

## XAN

I WAVED at Sage as I walked into The Lizard about a week after Chrome paid me a visit. Heading to my usual spot, I smiled as I realized how lucky I was to have a job, a place to live, and people like the Silvers to welcome me and keep me company. People like Chrome and the old clubs were in my past and I planned to keep them there.

Did I probably need to work in some healthier food somewhere in my diet?

Yeah, sure.

But part of the reason I loved the bar so much was because of the friendly faces and sense of belonging. It wasn't specifically a gay bar, it was just an open, welcoming place to spend time.

"Welcome to The Salty Lizard. What can I get for you?" a smooth, strong, teasing voice asked as a hand sat down a glass of water.

I nearly rocked my chair over when I glanced up to the source of the words and saw Chase standing there with a big ol' smile. "No shit? You're working here now?"

"First day; really it's just training." He grinned. "I'm working here *and* living upstairs. Crazy shit." He tapped his pen on a pad of paper. "You're actually the first person they've sent me out to wait on completely by myself. I've been *training* under Sage all day. I guess they figure you're easy and I can't screw it up too much." Chase winked. "Go easy, I'm a virgin."

I choked on a piece of ice.

Chase's ears burned red. "Virgin at taking orders. *New.* I'm new to this. Go easy." His head fell forward and he took a deep breath. "Jesus. I'm going to just stop talking. What do you want to eat?"

I smirked. "Oh, but this is quite entertaining. Feel free to go on." I waved my hand.

Chase rolled his eyes. "Are you eating something or not?"

"Well, no need to be rude," I teased. "I'd like the fish. Cheese, pickles, tartar sauce, please."

Chase was adorable as his tongue peeked out slightly from the corner of his mouth as he wrote down my order. He huffed. "Oh, um, it comes with fries. You want that or something else? You can do onion rings or tater tots for a dollar more."

"I'll take fries as long as you can hook me up with an extra cup of fry sauce." I waggled my brows.

He smiled as he wrote on the pad. "I think I can handle that. But if I get fired for giving extras, it will be your fault."

"I'll take that risk if it means more sauce." I winked.

Chase gave a quick smile and nod before walking away.

I chuckled. He hadn't asked me what I wanted to

drink. He'd either remember and come back, or I'd ask for a Coke when he brought my food. Either way, I would definitely be giving him a hard time.

About two minutes later, Chase came back to my table with a sheepish look. "Yeah, so, I guess you might want something to drink other than water."

I laughed. "It's really good water." I took a sip, never taking my eyes off him. *Holy shit*. Were we having a moment? It felt like a moment the way he stared at me and licked his lips. Nah, he was probably just embarrassed he'd forgotten my drink order. I coughed. "Um, I'll have a Coke, please."

I checked my texts and emails while Chase was gone.

"I've not messed up any orders today. Even though yours is my first solo shot, I'm thinking I got the Coke just right." He smiled as he placed the drink in front of me.

"So, what shifts are you working?" I stuck a straw in the fizzy liquid.

"Right now, Bode has me coming in at ten to work on set up and then working until six." Chase glanced over his shoulder as an order was called out. "Oh, that's your food." He rushed off to gather the order.

When he returned and placed the food on the table, I checked my phone. "So, you're actually off?" I had left the shop at six. I wasn't sweaty or dirty today, so I headed straight for dinner from work.

Chase bit his lip. "Um, I was getting ready to clock out when you walked in. I wanted to try an order on my own and I figured you wouldn't be too hard."

I smiled and popped a fry in my mouth. "Want to join me for dinner?"

The sincere look of gratitude that filled Chase's face caused my stomach to somersault.

He nodded. "Sure, let me clock out and grab something."

When he returned, he plopped a mini pizza and a bowl of Brussels sprouts down along with a water. "Thanks. I can eat in the back or upstairs, but this is better." His ears pinked and I began to think that his pale skin and penchant for blushing was quickly becoming a favorite of mine.

"Ten to six is what I work. Maybe you can be my dinner buddy." I spewed the offer before shoving the fish sandwich in my mouth and taking a huge bite. "You know, on nights you don't have other plans."

Chase nodded. "I think they mainly want me to work ten to six or eleven to seven. I guess I'm replacing the girl who had that shift before?"

"Yeah, I think it was Nikki or Vicki or something. Bode said she graduated and got a job in education or something." I took a drink before dipping fries in the sauce. I think it was safe to say I liked some fries with my sauce.

Chase wrinkled his nose. "I'll visit Aunt Ginny in the mornings or maybe some evenings if she's feeling up to it. But, other than helping out with Rosie, I don't exactly have a happenin' social life."

I snorted. "Maybe because you say things like *happenin' social life*," I teased. "Rosie's in school?"

"Yeah, I've been helping Sage get her and Oliver to school. I think Sage is going to start volunteering at the school since I'll be here most days." Chase forked a sprout and popped it in his mouth with a moan. "How do they make these so good?" He chewed and swallowed. "The good thing is they don't really *need* me on weekends. They've got some employees who requested weekend shifts and since I'm available through the week, it works perfectly.

"Well, if you've got free evenings or weekends that aren't booked with dates or whatever, we should hang." I shrugged and attempted to be as nonchalant as possible. Why was I so interested in Chase and I becoming friends? Was I really that fucking lonely?

*I think you know the answer to that.*

I pushed the thought away. "You play video games?"

Chase scoffed. "Definitely no *dates* and, yes, I play video games. You?"

I nodded. "I've got an Xbox One and a PS4."

"Whoa, look at you. Like a professional gamer and shit," Chase teased.

"The Xbox One was something I picked up at a pawn shop. The PS4 was my first big purchase after I started working at Whitfield's. What do you play?" I took another bite of my sandwich.

"NBA games, Mortal Kombat, and Call of Duty are great. Or they *were*. I haven't gotten to play anything for a long time. Used to play with my squad, but my former roommate was more a PC gamer. I didn't have the money for a system and he wasn't cool with giving up the TV for me to hook up a system even if I had one." Chase finished a slice of pizza, but left the crust. "So, I'm rusty, but I'd love to play sometime."

I opted to leave the comment about no dates alone. For now. "What's wrong with the crust?"

Chase shrugged. "I don't know. It's a good handle, but I've never liked most pizza crust."

"Such a child. Do you pick the crusts off your peanut butter and jelly, too?" Teasing Chase was quickly becoming a favorite pastime. Especially if it made him blush.

"Guilty. I can't stand that top crust. So papery." He chuckled. "You'd think a big, bad soldier would be okay with eating a little crust, but not me."

We finished our meal over friendly chatter.

"Can you grab my bill?" I reached for my wallet.

Chase nodded. "I'll ring you up."

I followed him to the register and handed over my card once Chase had pulled up my bill. He got very serious as he entered numbers and finalized my purchase. I signed the receipt and added a generous tip—not creepy generous, just a normal generous tip like I'd give anyone who provided good service.

"You don't need to tip me." Chase chuckled and blushed.

"You waited on me and provided a service. You deserve a tip." I shrugged.

"It's going to be weird if you're eating here all the time and tipping me."

"We'll work it so you're not my server, just my dinner partner. How's that?" I raised a brow.

Chase nodded. "That works."

We walked out of The Lizard after saying goodbyes and stood awkwardly on the sidewalk for a bit.

"Well, once you feel like you're in a groove with the job and whatnot, holler and we can set up some time to play." I pulled out my phone. "Put your number in."

Chase smirked and punched in his number. "I'll hold you to the gaming. Pizza, beer, and Call of Duty is like my dream date."

He froze and his eyes went wide.

"Not like a *date*. I meant more like a playdate." His face turned even redder. "Shit, that's no better. A dream night, dream get together." Chase dropped his head forward and sighed. "Fuuuuck." He took a deep breath. "Sounds like a good time and I'm looking forward to it."

I laughed as he stalked toward the back of the building where I assumed he'd go up to his new room. Was it weird I wanted to see where he lived? Yeah, weird.

As I walked back to my place, I texted Chase.

*Me: Thanks for eating dinner with me tonight. Looking forward to our playdate.*

    *Chase: Fuck off.*

    *Chase: But yeah, me too.*

---

## 11

## CHASE

THE FIRST MORNING I went with Sage to take Rosie and
Oliver to school, I was overwhelmed with the weirdest
feeling of wanting to stay with Rosie. Sage said she did
great in school, so me wanting to stay and protect her and
help there was just strange. I didn't tell Sage about
wanting to stay with my sister, but I think he got the idea,
because—after Rosie showed me everything she wanted
me to see and introduced me to her teacher and the class
fish—Sage lured me away with the promise of coffee and
pastries.

We ended up at The Silver and Gold Creative, the art
studio where Benji and Rhys worked. Well, they worked
there, but they also owned it. I immediately fell in love
with the place. What was not to like? Coffee, tea, and
pastries in a comfy little nook, amazing artwork, two
friendly—and, yes, super attractive—guys, and two great
dogs. Bear and Brawn were big and goofy, but they were
surprisingly calm in the studio. They were the types of

dogs that looked like they could clear shelves and make a mess, but they pretty much just lounged around. Even when they came sniffing for snacks, they were pretty subdued.

"We totally lucked out with their temperaments. They love a good walk or jog, but they're pretty chill most of the time." Rhys gave Bear a pat on the head.

"Do any of the customers balk at dogs being in the studio?" I asked as I petted Brawn.

"Not really. We've been bringing them in with us since they were tiny. We have a couple people whose kids are afraid of big dogs, so we make sure Bear and Brawn are in the back or we let the kids come around slowly."

"Hey, we did come to say hi, but we also came to see if you have any boxes." Sage coaxed Bear into shaking and gave him a treat.

"We did?" I glanced at Sage.

"You need to move, right?" Sage raised his brows.

"Oh, right."

"You're moving? Wait, do I even know where you live now?" Benji frowned.

I laughed. "I'm pretty far south of town."

"But, he's now our newest roommate," Sage announced.

"No kidding?" Rhys asked. "Awesome."

"Wow, that's great. Sage and Bode are pretty great. Not as great as I was as a roommate, but you'll like them." Benji winked. "And you get to live with a sister you didn't even know existed? Even better."

We gathered several boxes from the back of the studio.

"Figured we'd take these and some tape and go load up

your stuff." Sage glanced my way as we walked back to the apartment. "If you're up for that?"

"I'd love to, but my car crapped out and I was borrowing Todd's car but he came and got it." I frowned. "I could probably ask Ginny to use her car, but I don't know if I can get it today."

"Bode's got a truck. We'll take it and get all the moving taken care of. That way you can get moved in before you start working. I'm guessing you'll be able to start within a week." Sage led me to the back of the building where a truck I hadn't even paid attention to was parked. "Throw those in the back. I'll go get tape and rope."

"Better get a plastic bag if you're planning to abduct me," I joked.

Sage laughed and ran up the stairs. When he came back down, he stuck his head in the back door of The Lizard. "We're going to go pack up Chase's stuff. Love you!"

I climbed into the truck after Sage unlocked it.

"Put the address in my map." Sage handed me his phone.

After I typed in the address, he placed his phone in a holder on the dash.

"So, I was thinking. That Todd guy gave you until the end of the month, right? Had you already paid this month's rent?" Sage pulled the truck out of the tight parking spot and headed south.

"Yeah, I paid rent on the first."

"Okay, good. So, you don't owe him anything. We're going to give you the first month free."

"What?" I jerked my eyes from the road to look at Sage. "Why?"

"We talked about it. Figure you may need the money for moving expenses and whatnot. Didn't know if you'd need new shoes or jeans for work. Maybe toiletries and stuff." Sage gave me a smile. "Just didn't want you stressing the first month of rent."

My throat tightened and tears threatened. "Why are you guys doing this? A job? A place to stay? You're already doing a great thing for Ginny and Rosie. Why me?"

Sage was quiet for a bit. "Bode's dad never believed in him. My parents weren't the greatest. I was never good enough. Bode is where he is now because people gave him a chance. I'm where I'm at now because people gave me a chance and helped me out." He shrugged. "In a lot of ways, we know what it's like to be in your position. People helped us, we're helping you. When you're able, you can pay it forward and help someone else."

I had to turn away and watch out the window for three hard swallows as I composed myself. I turned back around. "Thank you. I'll definitely pay it forward."

"Damn, that was the perfect opportunity to mess with you." Sage snapped his fingers. "Should have told you we were planning to bring you in as our sex slave or something."

I turned huge eyes his way.

Sage cracked up. "Wow, your face is priceless. Can you imagine if you'd not known I was joking?" He wiped at tears in his eyes. "Truly, I'm just giving you shit. Just take the kindness and pass it along when you can."

"You're a nut." I shook my head. "A very generous nut, but still." I settled into the seat and allowed the warmth of a good situation to wash over me.

* * *

I got all my stuff moved into my new place and spent a few days helping with Rosie and training at The Lizard. In the evenings, I played with Oliver and Rosie until bedtime. Then I headed back down for more learning in the bar.

A week after they offered me the place to live and a job, I officially started at The Salty Lizard on the ten to six shift instead of earlier mornings or later nights.

At the end of my first day, Xan walked in and I nearly tripped over my tongue. I was getting ready to clock out when he walked through the door and I made a split-second decision to wait on him.

"I've got this one," I told Sage as I grabbed a glass of water. I felt Sage's smile as I headed toward Xan's table with my notepad at the ready. "Welcome to The Salty Lizard. What can I get for you?" I placed the ice water on his table.

If I thought my tongue got in the way when Xan walked in, I lost all control of it when he glanced up at me and smiled. From that exact moment until I rushed away from him after our shared dinner, I easily said about ten stupid things. I'd been yelled at by commanding officers in the past, but nothing prepared me for how much Xan would fuck up my head and my mouth.

*How much do you think he could fuck up your mouth?*

And thoughts like that were messing with me as well. *Fuck.*

I can't say the thought of being with a guy had *never* crossed my mind. But I couldn't stop my stupid head and dick from obsessing about Xan. It needed to stop. He seemed like a great guy and had invited me to eat dinner with him and come over to play games. I couldn't fuck it up with some crazy thoughts about what it would be like to kiss him. Or any of the other demented ideas floating around in my head.

With my head in the gutter and my tongue out of control, I realized quickly that I couldn't string together the simplest of sentences around Xan. But I was already looking forward to our nightly dinners and meeting up for some gaming.

\* \* \*

"I think your date is here," Bode teased as he filled a beer at the tap.

"Shut up," I hissed and my cheeks heated. "He's not my date. I'm not against dating guys, but I don't even know how *I'm* feeling toward him, let alone how he's feeling toward me." I crunched up my face as I looked at him. "How do you know I might even like him?"

Bode laughed quietly. "Man, it's written all over your face and has been since the first day Sage introduced the two of you." He shook his head. "Plus, you kinda admitted it, remember?"

I sighed as I punched my number on the screen to clock out. "For all I know, he's as straight as straight can be. Hell, until recently, I hadn't even really taken the time or given a shit enough to think about myself being anything but straight."

"Well, Sage and I are always around to listen if you ever want to chat about that or anything else." Bode put his arm around my shoulders and spoke low as he glanced toward Xan. "Straight or bi or gay or whatever, I think you two found each other at the perfect time in your lives. You're both somewhat new around here. You both had a pretty shitty upbringing. You're both starting anew. And you both seem to need a friend." He jostled me a bit. "You've got the whole Silver crew, but I think you and Xan could be just what the other needs." He gave me a little shove with his hip. "Now, go enjoy your dinner. Maybe sometime you can invite Xan upstairs..." he paused.

My eyes went wide.

"...to *cook* him something *other* than bar food. Like vegetables or something. Get your head out of the gutter." Bode winked. "I'm sure the kids would love a guest for dinner." He grabbed a towel to wipe the bar. "I know Xan's got a checkered past, but Bay ran a background check and it was clear. Bay and Kyson trust him completely, so I do, too."

I tried not to think about Bode saying my face clearly showed that I was developing a *thing* for Xan as I walked toward the table. I immediately lost all thoughts of actual conversation pieces when I sat down. "Hey," I blurted.

Xan's eyes crinkled and he attempted to hide a smile. "Hey, yourself. How was your shift?"

Thank God Xan seemed to be able to carry on a decent conversation.

I smiled. "Good. Didn't mess up any orders. It's not like the orders here are fancy, or the customers demanding, I'm just always worried I'll get something wrong."

Xan nodded. "I get that. But a mess up isn't the worst thing in the world. At least not here. Forgetting the drink, serving fries instead of onion rings, not putting tartar sauce on the side, all of those things are easily remedied."

"Yeah, I guess. I'll remember that if I ever forget your fry sauce." I winked.

"Forget my fry sauce? Blasphemy." Xan held a hand to his chest as if wounded. "You were in the Army, right?" When I nodded, he went on. "I'm guessing mess-ups there were a little more important?"

"Yeah, definitely no fun getting yelled at by a commanding officer. Luckily, I was in a position that didn't have a lot to do with life or death situations. I'm not sure I could have handled that stress."

Darryl came over at that time and took our orders.

"But you liked the Army overall?" Xan asked.

"Yeah, it was good to me mostly." I flexed my leg under the table as an achiness surged through it. "Really wish I could have stayed in, but the knee took me out." I raised and lowered a shoulder. "I was really bummed about it for a while. Got pretty down. I'd still love to make the Army my career, but I'm kinda hoping things are starting to look up."

Xan smiled. "I definitely get *that*." He took a drink from the soda Darryl had dropped off. "Sometimes I wonder if I would have been successful in the military. Would have kept me out of trouble, but by eighteen, I was already in so deep with the bad crowd, I'm not sure they would have taken me."

I pursed my lips. "Probably would have. They take

pretty much anyone. Save a lot of messed up kids from trouble. Turn them around."

"Always wondered if it would have helped me." Xan tapped his fingers on the table. "Then again, my past makes me who I am. Not proud of some of the stuff I did. And I'm learning to accept that a lot of bad shit was done to me—it's amazing what a kid assumes is okay when they don't have any good role models in their life. But I'm like you, it feels like things may be turning around for me. Maybe it's a little late, but better late than never."

I cocked my head to the side. "How old are you?"

"How old do you think I am?"

"I'm twenty-eight, so I'm guessing right around that." I raised a brow.

"Thirty. Not bad. Maybe you could work for a carnival and guess ages," he teased.

Our food arrived and I breathed in deeply. "Smells good."

"See? This food is addictive. Tell me the truth, they put crack in the grease to keep people coming back for more, right?" Xan squirted ketchup on his burger.

"Maybe someday, I'll cook a real meal and invite you to partake." I popped a tator tot in my mouth.

"Will there be fry sauce?" Xan asked around a bite of burger.

"Veggies and actual food don't need fry sauce." I frowned. "Only problem with this plan is that I'm not really that great of a cook. I can pop a frozen pizza in the oven, microwave a burrito, heat up soup. But I don't actually have a repertoire of recipes."

"I'm possibly even slightly less skilled than you. Maybe

we can cook together and make a vegetable laden masterpiece." Xan dipped an onion ring into fry sauce.

"Vegetable laden?" I wrinkled my nose. "Let's not get too crazy. I'm thinking like a nice main dish, a side of veggies, a bread, a dessert. Or we could do spaghetti. That's got tomatoes, it counts as veggies, right?"

"Add a salad and we've got a regular garden of healthy food." Xan winked.

"So, what do you mostly do at Whitfield's?" I asked before taking a sip of Coke.

"Mechanic stuff mostly. Every so often, I'll help on the sales floor with merchandise or bikes, but Bay does most of the actual bike sales." Xan took another bite of his sandwich and chewed before speaking. "I like getting to learn the detailing and paint jobs, but my skills are in rebuilding and repair." He shrugged. "Since I'm new, I get the jobs that aren't appointments or requests. Some of the guys have regulars. I'm getting to a point where I may have two or three requests a month. The rest of the time, I'm working on what others can't or won't."

"You like it?"

"Love it." Xan nodded. "I was a fucked-up mess as a kid and teen, but motorcycles have always been my thing."

"What was fucked-up?" I cocked my head.

"Bio dad left for his *real* family, Mom couldn't handle it and abandoned me. Spent most of my time in and out of foster care. Got mixed up with some really rough crowds."

"What is it about motorcycles?" I found I wanted to hear more and more about Xan with each passing moment.

He was quiet for a moment. "They don't leave you,

they don't abuse you, they don't use you as their bitch. Bikes are just there. Nothing better than firing a big ol' bitch up and listening to her purr; figure out what's bothering her and how to fix it. Get her back to top condition and feeling good."

I smiled softly. "Sounds like you've found yourself the perfect job with Bay."

Xan nodded. "I'd be happy doing what I'm doing for the rest of my life."

"That's great." I sighed. "I'm really loving working here and I'm grateful for the opportunity Sage and Bode have given me. I don't know that I want to wait tables in a bar the rest of my life, but for the time being, it's good for me. Money, place to stay, new friends, I've got what I need."

We ate in silence for a while.

"So, your aunt was your sister's mom for a while, but now she can't take care of Rosie?" Xan asked. "Sorry, don't mean to be nosey."

"It's okay. Yeah, my mom was an alcoholic drug addict —she's the reason why I left home at eighteen and never looked back—she got pregnant with Rosie, wouldn't stop the drugs and drinking, Ginny was given custody. Then Ginny was diagnosed with cancer. Now Sage and Bode have Rosie. And I have a sister I never knew about. It's crazy."

"How's Ginny?"

I took a deep breath. "I think she's a lot sicker than she lets on. But she's not doing chemo or radiation—says this option allows her to have more good days with Rosie —I guess because the cancer is too far spread. She doesn't seem to want to talk to me much about it. Wants to focus on Rosie and me and only the good."

"That's rough. I'm sorry. You were close to her as a kid?"

"Yeah, she was more a mom to me than my actual mother. Didn't get to see her often. Hated to leave without contacting her, but I had no choice." My eyes stung with threatening tears. "Really glad she found me. Her determination brought me here and I'm forever grateful." I shook my head to break from the emotion. "I like your ink. How many tattoos do you have?"

Xan took the bait and glanced down at his arms. "Honestly, I've lost track of how many I have. A lot of them were separate pieces that are now connected into larger pieces."

"Are they just on your arms?" My gut gave a little clench at the thought of the beautiful marks traveling all over his body.

"Nah, arms, chest, stomach, back, legs. Never wanted any on my neck or face, but everywhere else was open game." Xan studied one on his inner wrist. "This one, the dagger right here, it was my very first. Got it on a dare and was hooked on ink from that moment on. Couple of them were stick and poke types."

My eyes grew wide with my head clearly in the gutter.

Xan laughed. "It's an old style of tattooing, dirty boy. A sharp object and ink are all that's needed. Some look a lot better than others."

My face heated. "Do they all have a meaning?" I allowed my eyes to roam over his arms as I imagined what the rest of his body looked like covered in ink.

"A lot of the first ones don't. They were just inked for

the hell of it, letting friends use me as a practice canvas, just for the momentary thrill." He bent his elbow to look at one of the designs. "Over the past few years, I've been more intentional in the designs. I've done some of the original sketches myself. I'll need to find someone here in Indy to do my next one." He lifted his eyes to meet mine. "What about you? Get the customary military ink with the rest of your squad?"

I shivered and shook my head. "Hell no. I'm terrified of needles."

Xan's eyes went wide. "No shit?"

"Yeah, like they nearly had to sedate me to get me through the vaccines and boosters I needed to enlist." I gritted my teeth. "Just the thought of a shot or bloodwork has had me heading into a panic attack in the past. I've tried to get better about it, but I still break into a cold sweat."

"Wow, I've heard of people scared of needles, but I don't know that I've ever known someone who hates them that much." Xan cocked his head. "Is it the pain?"

"The pain, the anticipation, the metal puncturing my skin, all of it." I shuddered. "I don't even like talking about it. And the thing that sucks is I've always wanted a tattoo, but I don't think I could ever sit through it knowing needles are breaking through my skin." I took a long drink of water in hopes of calming the anxious feeling beating through my chest.

"Well, if you ever decide to do it, I'll go with you." Xan's eyes caught mine. "For real. It's not super painful and if you can get into a zone, it's almost therapeutic. At least, it has been for me. I'd hold your hand and keep you distracted. No pressure, just know the offer is there."

I took a deep breath. "Thanks. I doubt it will ever come to that. But I appreciate it."

* * *

Xan and I spent the next couple of weeks eating dinner together every evening. I found myself anxiously awaiting dinnertime just to see my new friend. And I resented the first few weekends because I didn't get to spend time with Xan; I was ready to set up those gaming dates—get togethers—but we hadn't gotten around to it. We texted constantly about random and unimportant shit. But it was nice to have that connection.

I'd convinced myself that I'd rather have Xan as a friend than screw up whatever we'd been building by trying to make it into more than friendship. And Xan seemed to be on the same page as he never once appeared to want more than exactly what we had. And I was good with that.

Honestly.

Okay, maybe not *good* with it. But I accepted it. I'd gone a long time without romantic relationships or sexually fulfilling relationships. Did I like sex? Yeah, it was okay. Maybe I'd just never had it with the right people. But I could totally rely on my right hand for the time being if it meant getting to spend time with Xan. Maybe sex just wasn't that important to me. And did I want my first foray into a buried bisexuality to be with someone I wanted to keep as a friend? No. Well, I wasn't one-hundred percent on that one, but it seemed best to keep the two separate.

Which meant I *really* needed to stop thinking about Xan naked; needed to stop thinking about sex with Xan.

As I clocked out, I checked my phone. Usually Xan texted if he was going to be late, but there was no message. I frowned.

"Where's your boy?" Bode asked.

I tossed him an exasperated look. "He's *not* my boy." I shrugged. "And I don't know." I sat at the bar to wait for a moment and sipped at a vodka tonic the bartender had made too strong for a customer. I wasn't a heavy drinker, usually stuck to beer and cider, but I didn't want to waste the drink. And the alcohol would maybe help ease the disappointment if Xan didn't show up.

Bode glanced my way and disappeared for a bit. He returned a while later as I was finishing the vodka. He held up a big brown paper bag boasting The Salty Lizard logo. "Talked to Bay. Said your boy," he paused and held up a hand of surrender, "your *friend* smashed his thumb at work today. Sent him home a bit ago to ice it and keep it elevated." Bode shook the bag. "Figured you could take him dinner. I put in food for both of you."

I pulled my wallet out. "Thanks. That's nice of you."

"On the house, a get well for Xan."

I knew arguing was pointless, so I took the bag. "Do you know where he lives?"

"Yeah, I'll text you the address, but you're going to go down three blocks to the left when you leave here, turn left, go two more blocks, turn right and Whitfield's is there. He's upstairs. May have to buzz him to get in the door, I'm not sure anyone will be at the shop to let you in."

I thanked Bode again and headed out the door toward Xan's place.

As I walked, my phone buzzed twice. The first message was Bode sending the address. The second text was Xan.

**Xan**: *Gonna have to miss dinner. Smashed the shit out of my thumb today. Hurts like a motherfucker. It's super swollen and blood is filling up under the nail.*

**Me**: *I'm on my way with get well food from Bode. Bay told him about your injury. Can you let me in?*

**Xan**: *Wow, that's super nice. Just buzz at the back when you get here. Sorry I won't be great company, but I'd love to have you hang out while I cry about my damn thumb.*

I smiled and attempted to push down the fluttery feeling in my chest. I was going to Xan's place. He was happy I was going to hang out. That's what friends did. That's all it was.

I found Whitfield's easily and buzzed at the back door. The door clicked and I headed up the back stairs.

I recognized the pain in Xan's eyes the moment he pulled the door open.

I winced as I took in his ice-wrapped hand stuck up in the air as he attempted to reduce the swelling. "Dude, you look like you're about to pass out."

He gritted his teeth and nodded. "It's bad. Throbbing like a bitch. That food smells great, but I'm not sure I can eat."

"Let me take a look," I commanded as I sat the bag down on the table. "Do you have a match or a lighter?"

Xan blanched but nodded.

"A needle?"

"I thought you were scared of needles?" Xan asked.

"Used on *me*, yes. But I think I can help if it's blood under your nail causing all the pain." I raised my brow. "You have a needle or not?"

Xan cringed but nodded. "Yeah." He side-eyed me. "But I'm suddenly very afraid."

# 12

---

## XAN

I'D BEEN an hour away from being done for the day. I was covered in grease, so I was going to run home and shower before meeting Chase for dinner. Our meals at The Lizard had become the highlight of my days, and that was saying a lot because I loved my job.

Damned Cliff had called me over to help him finish up a job. Not sure if the man didn't have the bike secured well or if it was just a freak shift, but the bitch slipped and something heavy came down on my thumb. The pain was so searing and quick, I didn't even get a chance to figure out what smashed me. Cliff, to his credit, got the damn bike up and off me quickly, but the damage had been done.

I'd gotten plenty of burns and scrapes in my years of working on motorcycles, but a smashed finger or thumb always seemed the worst. Cliff had grabbed me some ice and told Bay what happened. My boss took a look at the injury and sent me home. Told me to ice it, keep it up, and pop ibuprofen. As I left with every beat of my heart throbbing in my thumb, Bay called out. "You know you're going to need to relieve the pressure under that nail if it keeps building up."

After a quick shower and several ibuprofen, I'd wrapped new ice around my thumb and collapsed onto the couch. I checked the time and saw I was definitely late for dinner. *Damn it*. Was Chase waiting on me? Why did it do weird things to my insides to think of him waiting on me?

My stomach rolled with nausea from the pain—very likely way too much medication—and my head was pounding from clenching my teeth against the excruciating pain in my thumb. I knew the pain was getting worse because the blood was building up under the nail. But what was I going to do to release the pressure? Maybe I needed the emergency room. But that seemed like overkill for a smashed thumb.

When I finally swallowed the rising bile and texted Chase, I found I was a confusing mix of happy and dismayed he was coming over. Happy because that meant he was as bummed as me that I was missing our dinner. Happy because I was going to get to spend time with him. Dismayed because I knew I'd be crap company. Dismayed because I didn't want to look like a total whiner about a damn smashed thumb.

But before I knew it, Chase was buzzing at my door and I fought against the nausea and lightheadedness to let him in the door. Within moments, Chase had abandoned the delicious-smelling food and ushered me to the bathroom with requests for matches or a lighter and a needle. My head was kinda fuzzy, but fire and needles did not sound like a fun time.

"Sit down on the toilet. I'm going to gather supplies." Chase put down the toilet lid and rushed from the bathroom. He returned a moment later with a paper towel. "I'm going to look this up real quick and be sure a needle is the best thing to use." He pulled out his phone. "Where's the lighter?"

"Wait, you've never done this?" I clutched my injured hand to my chest.

"I've heard of it working, but no, I've not done it myself. Do you want your thumb to feel better or not?"

"Lighter is in the drawer next to the stove." I gritted my teeth as my thumb demonstrated its ability to replicate my heartbeat. I leaned forward and put my head between my knees as I waited for Chase.

"Hey, can you come into the kitchen? I think I have a better plan."

I took a deep breath and headed to the kitchen.

"Sit. I'm going to use a paperclip and your stove." Chase's eyes were glued to his phone as he gathered more paper towels since I'd left the others in the bathroom.

"My *stove*?" I couldn't help the high pitch near squeal my voice took on. "A paperclip and my stove? Can I opt out?"

Chase stood in front of my chair. "For someone who has over half his body covered in tattoos, you seem a bit squeamish."

"The tattoos weren't being applied to already excruciatingly painful areas of my body. And most of the artists had at least *some* experience. They weren't trying to ink me after hearing about it being done or watching a damn video." I scowled.

Chase rolled his eyes and took another glance at his

phone before putting it on the table. "Watch this while I gather everything."

I watched the video of a man who had been working in a shop and smashed his finger. His finger was swollen and the blood was definitely building under his nail. Honestly, my thumb was a lot more swollen and bruised than his, but I clenched my jaw and figured if this guy could do it, so could I.

"Okay, alcohol and cotton balls in the bathroom?" Chase asked.

I nodded and kept my eyes on the video as the guy attempted to heat a paperclip with a lighter. When that didn't work, he moved to his gas stove. The procedure went very quickly once the paperclip was hot enough and the man on the video said the relief was immediate. I took a deep breath. I was ready for this. "You gonna grab pliers? Toolbox is under the kitchen sink."

Within five minutes, Chase had cleaned my nail and the paperclip with alcohol. He turned on the overhead light and the stove light, had me move the chair near the stove, and gripped the clip with the pliers. "Put your hand on the paper towel," he commanded.

I did as I was told and stared at the fire as Chase cooked the unbent paperclip in the flame until it was glowing red. I took another deep breath and found myself immediately distracted from the process taking place before me as I caught a whiff of Chase's scent. He smelled like the bar, but under that was soap, deodorant, and just Chase. His body pressed against my shoulder as he leaned in to heat the paperclip and I couldn't help but press against him slightly.

Chase pulled the clip from the fire and placed the tip

against my nail. There was no more pain than what I'd already been dealing with and within seconds, my thumb exploded and blood flowed out of a tiny hole.

"Whoa!" Chase yelped and jerked back.

The relief was immediate, but the blood continued to pour from the opening for several moments. I let Chase concern himself with draining the blood and soaking it up with the paper towel as I slumped against the chair.

"Damn, you should have worn gloves." I sat up and scowled. "I mean, I don't have any infections. Bay requests bloodwork and a complete physical for work. All clear. But still…" I trailed off.

"No worries. I trust you enough to know you'd protect me if there was something I needed to know about." Chase pressed my thumb again. "Bode and Sage request bloodwork and a physical as well. Don't *have* to do the bloodwork, but the physical is a must. My results were clear."

"You did the bloodwork? Wow." I sighed as my heartbeat retreated from my thumb to my chest.

"Yeah, figured it was an important step toward my new start, so I had Ginny go with me." Chase shrugged. "When you have a cancer patient with you, it's kinda hard to complain about a quick stick and a few vials of blood."

I flexed my thumb and fingers. "Yeah, I can see that." A breath whooshed out of me. "That feels so much better. Gotta admit, I was scared of what you had planned, but that was amazingly helpful. Thank you."

"No problem. Probably still be sore, and you may lose the nail, but at least the extreme pain is gone." Chase gathered up the soiled paper towel and reached under the sink for disinfecting spray. After soaking the counter area, he washed his hands before wiping down the counter. "You feel like eating now?"

"I got to grab a quick shower after work. If you're going to hang for a bit, do you want to shower? I can give you some sweats and a t-shirt." I gestured toward the bathroom.

Chase started to protest, but he must have changed his mind because he nodded. "I'll be quick. Would be nice to get the greasy smell off my skin."

"I hear ya, different grease, but I feel the same after work some days." I grabbed a towel from the linen closet and tossed it to him. "I'll put some clothes on the sink for you."

After the shower turned on, I waited a full two minutes before retrieving a pair of sweats and a t-shirt. As I placed the clothes on the sink, purposely averting my eyes from the shower stall, I realized my thumb had oozed some blood and dripped on the t-shirt. "Hey, I bled on this shirt. There are pants here. Come out when you're done and I'll get you a shirt." Yeah, that didn't sound like a convenient ruse to see him without a shirt. My cock stirred.

Five minutes later, I'd managed to bleed all over my own shirt. I stripped it off and stood at the kitchen sink applying stain removing spray to both shirts. I turned quickly, almost as if I'd been caught doing something wrong, when Chase emerged from the bathroom. "Sorry, bled on my own shirt too. Give me a second." I attempted to look anywhere but at Chase's chest and abs, but my eyes were drawn to the pale skin, a light dusting of blond hair, the pink nipples, his navel, and the trail of hair that traveled under the waistband of his borrowed sweats.

*Fuck.*

When in the hell had I ever been so damn attracted to a man's fucking chest? I tore my eyes from his body and glanced at Chase's face.

Only to find his eyes glued to me. I knew he was taking in my bronze skin, the dark hair spread over my chest and abs, and the ink covering my body. My chest caught fire as my dick took immediate interest in Chase's eyes roaming all over me.

I cleared my throat. "Okay, hopefully those shirts can be saved. Let me grab you a shirt." I rinsed my hands and made my way to my drawer.

"Wait, we should wrap your thumb so you don't bleed on more clothes." Chase broke from his trance and moved closer to take my hand so he could inspect my thumb.

The heat from our bodies met between us and mixed in a tantalizing swirl of warmth that wrapped itself around us and kissed our skin. I struggled to breathe and my nostrils flared as I worked to control my reaction to Chase's proximity.

"There are bandages in the bathroom."

Chase gestured me toward the steamy room and I breathed through my mouth to avoid smelling my soap mixed with Chase still hanging heavy in the room.

*You idiot, it's your own soap. You smell it every day.*

But picturing Chase naked in my shower, soaping his skin, it was too much.

Chase rummaged through my drawers and broke me from my horny ridiculousness. "Here, use this tissue to squeeze some blood out one last time." He handed me a tissue while he opened several bandages.

I gently squeezed until no more blood appeared at the tiny hole. "Okay, I think it's good for now."

Chase tore a piece from the paper towel I'd left on the sink earlier. "I'm thinking put this under the bandages to soak up any oozing and also kinda protect it?"

I nodded.

He stood on my right as I faced the mirror. When he applied the folded cloth, I had to grit my teeth and hold my breath as he shifted and reached around me to grab a bandage on the left side of the sink. His warm skin skimmed over my back and I refused to believe that I felt a stiff nipple brush against me.

And then I made the mistake of glancing into the mirror.

Chase's eyes met mine for one tense moment before skittering away. His pale skin was flushed whether from a hot shower or desire and I was hit with a stupid need to feel his arms wrapped around me. Could I turn in his arms and pull his body tightly against mine?

Yeah, I could.

Did I want to?

Fuck yeah, I did.

How would Chase respond?

Well, that was the kicker. He looked like he might want to do exactly the same thing as I was thinking. But I didn't want to get it wrong.

Chase was my friend.

Aside from the Silver guys, Chase was my *only* friend. Sure, I got along with the guys at Whitfield's, but I didn't make dinner and gaming plans with them. I didn't look forward to seeing them every day.

I shifted against the sink in hopes of concealing the

tent growing in my pants. But moving from the sink pushed me backwards just enough that my hip grazed Chase and the unmistakable thick cock under his borrowed sweats.

*Fuck.*

*Fuck.*

*Fuck.*

I needed to breathe, but I worried I'd hyperventilate if I started gulping air the way my lungs craved. With my teeth clenched, my nostrils flared as I very slowly attempted to breathe without giving away that I was as turned on as Chase obviously was.

His chest and face were as red as I'd ever seen and he sputtered something about needing to finish up the bandages. Somehow, neither of us passed out from blood rushing to our dicks or from embarrassment.

Chase finished my thumb and tossed the trash. "Um, I'm going to try to salvage the food. Can you grab me a shirt?"

I kept my eyes averted from him and nodded with a cough. "Yeah, be right out. Probably best to do sandwiches in the microwave, fries or rings may do better in the oven for a bit."

Chase mumbled something that sounded like an agreement as he made a quick exit. I couldn't tear my eyes from the broad expanse of pale skin, trim waist, and tantalizing dimples that peeked from just under the waistband of his pants.

I swung the bathroom door closed with a bit too much force and winced as I leaned my forehead against the door. Deep breaths. Think of anything except Chase. I breathed through my nose and out my mouth.

*Fuck.*

Being attracted to a guy wasn't super new.

Being attracted to a guy I considered my friend—a friend I truly didn't know very well just yet—*was* new.

Being attracted to a guy in a situation where I could actually act upon the attraction—and found myself very much wanting to act—was completely new.

And fucking scary as hell.

Some of the guys at the shop had been giving me a rough time about not going to clubs and getting laid. I always scoffed and joked they didn't know what I was doing with my free time. But maybe the reason I'd had no desire to hook up with girls from clubs was because I was discovering—maybe *uncovering* was a better word—an interest in men that I'd pushed away long ago.

Did I find *every* guy attractive?

No. No one found every person they saw attractive.

Did I find some men attractive?

I took a deep breath.

Yes.

Did I find Chase attractive?

Fuck, yes. No question.

Was I willing to screw up our friendship for that attraction?

No. Not a chance.

The thought of losing Chase had effectively deflated my hard-on and I quickly took a piss before emerging from the bathroom.

The sight that greeted me—Chase looking all domestic in my kitchen as he peered into the window of the oven with his amazing ass and beautiful skin on display—was enough to send me back into the bathroom to jack off.

How could the thought of Chase in my kitchen, cooking for me—okay, warming up bar food—like a *partner* would, how did *that* threaten to get me hard again?

"You want a t-shirt or hoodie?" I cleared my throat.

Chase stood and turned my way. "Hoodie if you've got it."

I returned with a hoodie for him as I pulled one over my head. "Thanks again for doctoring my thumb. Feels a lot better." I pulled fry sauce from the bag. "Damn, how can reheating grease smell so good?"

Chase yanked the sweatshirt over his head. "Right? They sent cheeseburgers and onion rings and Brussels sprouts." He slid the onion rings and sprouts from the oven before opening the microwave to produce two burgers. "Probably won't be *as* good as fresh from their kitchen, but totally acceptable."

We took our food to the couch and settled in to eat and watch whatever was on TV. About halfway through the food, I had an idea that would maybe allow me to keep Chase around for a bit longer.

"So," I held up my injured thumb, "I don't think I'll be doing much gaming for at least a few days."

He chuckled. "I guess I won't try to take advantage."

"You up for a movie? Find something on Netflix?" I picked up the remote and raised my brows as I waited for him to reply.

Chase bit his lip and he hesitated like he was going to say no, but then he shrugged and nodded. "Sure."

We decided on some spy movie.

It wasn't a great movie and it seemed to drag on and on. As I found myself falling asleep, I gathered all the trash from dinner and took it to the kitchen. When I returned, I switched off the light and took my seat next to Chase again.

About twenty minutes later, after I'd jerked awake no less than three times, I felt Chase's head flop onto my shoulder. I expected him to startle awake, but he didn't.

Did I finish the movie?

Wake Chase and tell him to go home?

Neither of those sounded good.

So, I shoved a pillow under my left side and leaned against the arm of the couch. A short nap wouldn't hurt anything.

I woke later with a cramp in my leg and a heavy weight on my hip. I immediately realized Chase had cuddled farther down while we slept. Aside from the stiffness in my leg, his closeness was perfect and welcome. I turned my head to stare down at his light blond hair. Never before had I been as comfortable around a man as I was with Chase. We weren't purposely cuddling on the couch, but we'd obviously been drawn to each other in our sleep. And, if I was being honest with myself, I didn't want to move or lose Chase's presence; more than anything I wanted to wrap my arm around him and pull him closer.

The moment was broken before I could decide one way or the other. Chase stirred and then froze. I felt his body tense and the air immediately became awkward. So as not to let on that I knew he'd been asleep on me, I stayed still for a moment while he eased up off me and stretched. Only then did I pretend to wake. I shifted and rubbed my eyes.

"Damn man, sorry. Did I fall asleep?" I stretched my leg and groaned as the muscle complained. I hoped I was coming off as nonchalant despite desperately wanting Chase plastered against my side again.

He chuckled. "Yeah, I think we both did. Sorry about that."

"No worries, I guess the movie kinda put us to sleep." I stood from the couch and Chase followed. "Next time, it's time for you to get your ass handed to you with some gaming. I'm thinking Mortal Kombat all day long."

"Sounds perfect. But I'm pretty sure I'm better than you're thinking I am." He elbowed me. "I better get going. You going to work tomorrow?"

"Unless something weird happens with my thumb overnight, yeah." My injury was sore, but wasn't terribly painful any longer. "You want to plan on gaming on Saturday?"

"Sounds good." Chase hovered by the door as if he had something he wanted to say, but he just sighed and pressed his lips together. "You planning on dinner tomorrow?"

"Sure thing. See you then." Why did I want to pull him into a hug? God, I *had* to get whatever this was under control.

# 13

## CHASE

WAKING up last night to find I'd shifted to lean on Xan at some point during the movie was equally amazing and terrifying.

The way I immediately felt safe, connected, and *right* brought a warmth to my chest that I never wanted to lose. But those same feelings also scared the shit out of me. Would Xan freak out when he woke to find me plastered against him?

Luckily, I made it out of the situation fairly easily and now had dinner and gaming with Xan to look forward to.

After my visit with Aunt Ginny that morning, I also had a question for him. It was a big favor, but I had an idea that Xan would think it was great. Ginny had suggested I take advantage of a great offer the son of one of her friends was advertising. Even if Xan wasn't on board, it felt like something I couldn't pass up.

"You could probably ask Xan to help you," Ginny suggested with a bit of a sly smile that morning when we were walking back to her room from the cafeteria.

I narrowed my eyes at her. "Why do you look like that? What are you thinking?"

"Not anything specific, really." She shrugged and opened the door to her room. "I know that you and Xan eat dinner together every night."

I crossed my arms and leaned against the doorway. "How do you know that?"

Ginny waved a hand in the air and made her way to the refrigerator to offer me a bottle of water. "Oh, you know. I hear things. Did I tell you that Bay's grandmother, Millie, and his mother, Bonnie, come visit me often even if I'm not at the bar? And I see Bode and Sage quite a bit, even when you're not around. So, I hear things."

I took a quick drink before pressing my lips together. "Xan is a good friend."

Ginny bit back a smile and nodded. "Did I ever tell you how pissed your mom got when I told her I was a lesbian?"

I choked on the water. "Say what?" I knew my eyes were about to bug out of my head.

Ginny smiled triumphantly. "I slept with quite a few men and women before I realized I was a lot more homosexual than bisexual. I was nearing forty when I told Kathryn I liked women. She nearly had a cow. Told me I was disgusting and trying way too hard to convince people I was an independent, free-spirited badass." She snorted. "Because obviously all lesbians are independent, free-spirited, and badass." Ginny cocked her head. "I mean, *I* am all of those things, but I didn't claim to be a lesbian just to prove I was those things."

"Wow. She never told me." I frowned. "And neither did you."

Ginny shrugged. "There was no reason to tell you when you were younger. I knew my sister would never let me bring a girlfriend over. Plus, I didn't really date. It was more like I had women in each layover city. I loved the setup. I never wanted to settle down or give my heart to just one person."

I allowed her words to soak in and my chest tightened. "I think I'm a *give my heart to one person* type. But how do I know who's the right person?" I immediately thought of Xan. Of course, I did.

Ginny cocked her head and smiled. "I think it's one of those things where you'll know when you know. The closest I ever came to falling hard and forever was with a woman who made every relationship and hookup of my past seem dull in comparison. She was so different. Made me feel more, made me want more, made me realize I'd been missing something the whole time I'd thought I was happy and content."

My mouth turned down at the corners. "Why didn't you make something more with her?"

Ginny's eyes sparkled with unshed tears. "She was killed shortly before I planned to leave the airline and spend the rest of my life with her."

My throat clenched. "I'm sorry, that's terrible."

"Her name was Rose." Ginny chuckled. "When I suggested the name *Rosie* to your mom, she had no clue I wanted to name the baby after my dead lesbian lover. I like to think it was a great little bit of creativity on my part. Kathryn never knew and Rosie carries the name of an amazing woman. I always thought the name would keep a piece of Rose with me forever; didn't plan on it being something I'd leave Rosie with at such a young age." She sighed and I saw the wince of pain.

"Are you okay? Do you need a nurse?"

Ginny shook her head. "No, I'll be fine. Just need some rest. I have therapy later."

I resisted the urge to glance at the clock in her room. It was barely late morning and she was already dealing with pain and exhaustion? My heart lurched. "Let me get you settled in bed."

Ginny moved to the bed and allowed me to pull up the covers. "Thank you, dear boy. I'm so very glad to know Rosie has you along with Bode and Sage." She patted my hand. "Don't push away something with Xan just because it's not what you expected. Be open to the unexpected; sometimes our expectations and plans keep us from something amazing. Don't lose out on something amazing." Ginny's eyes drooped as she finished speaking.

I leaned forward and kissed her forehead. "I love you. I'll visit again soon. Maybe pick you up to come see Rosie."

Ginny's physical health had taken a slight turn for the worse lately and she wasn't allowing herself to drive. Partly because she didn't trust her body and partly because she was often on pain medication. Bode, Sage, and I had been taking turns picking her up so she could come see Rosie. Ginny often spent time at The Lizard talking to Bonnie and Millie. I was glad Ginny had some friends.

As I drove Sage's car back to the apartment, I tried to push away the ache in my heart. I wasn't going to have Ginny forever and it hurt to think I was losing her when I'd just gotten her back.

Taking a deep breath and wiping my eyes, I headed into the bar to ask Bode if he'd be willing to help me go pick up my surprise. If he was willing, I'd present the idea to Xan at dinner.

* * *

"So, if I were to have a total fixer-upper motorcycle, would you happen to know anyone who would want to help me fix it up?" I bit the corner of my lip and lifted my brow.

Xan stopped chewing and eyed me over his tenderloin sandwich for a moment before his face broke into a huge smile. "No shit? You got a bike?"

I held up a hand. "Okay, before you get too excited, I think it's fixable. However, it's *very* much in need of fixing. The guy said the engine just needs a good servicing, so that sounded somewhat promising. I know it needs a lot of repair and replacing along with body work." I winced. "But, in my defense, the guy just gave it to me as long as I'd pick it up and get it off his property. I guess it might be too far gone, but I'd love to have you check it out. If you think it's doable, maybe you could help me?"

Xan put his food down and leaned back in his chair. With one hand crossed over his midsection and a hand on his chin, he cocked his head and appeared to be thinking hard. "Spend time with a friend doing something I adore even more than fry sauce?"

I chuckled. "Maybe decide *after* you see the bike."

"I'll take a look at it, but I have to warn you that I'm pretty determined once I set my mind to something. If your girl gives me even the slightest indication of being repairable, I'm going to be totally on board." He rubbed his hands together. "Have you seen her? Ohhhh, please tell me she's a complete diamond in the rough that just needs polishing."

"I saw a picture. It was recognizable as a motorcycle. Looked like *she'd* been through hell and back. But the guy said he wanted to give it away to someone willing to fix her up rather than just selling her for parts." I held up a finger in warning. "But remember, I have next to *zero* experience with motorcycles aside from riding them a few times. I figure if it was free, and I'd only be out the money for parts and such, maybe it was a worthwhile project to take on."

"I love it. I'm definitely in. When can you bring it to the shop?" Xan's eyes sparkled like brown gemstones reflecting the sun.

"Couple of questions first." I popped a few fries in my mouth.

Xan took another bite of tenderloin and waited.

"How much will parts cost?"

Xan wrinkled his nose. "Hard to say. I can get them pretty cheap, but it's going to depend on what she needs. A lot of bike enthusiasts buy what they can when they can and fix things slowly as able."

I nodded. "I can do that. Save money for the more expensive parts as time goes along." I took a drink. "Will Bay be okay with you working on my bike at the shop? Do you think he'll charge?"

Xan shook his head. "Nah, everyone can have a bike at the shop as long as we keep it cleaned up and move it to the garage if the bays get too full. I don't have my bike in the bays, so yours can take the spot."

I bit my lip. "How much will you charge?"

Xan laughed. "You're kidding right?"

I scowled. "I'm asking you to give up your time and put a lot of effort into fixing something that you'll get no monetary benefit from."

Xan dunked an onion ring in fry sauce. "First, you're asking me to do something I absolutely love. No payment needed. Second, we already hang out; might as well be productive with our time. No payment needed. Third, if you'll let me take pics and use it to advertise my work, it may end up bringing me monetary benefits. *No payment needed*."

"Do you think we could sell it? Maybe fix it up and split the profit?" I scratched at my chin before eating the last of my club sandwich.

Xan nodded. "We could. But do you not want it to ride?"

"Fixing it up and making it my own was the original plan, but I can see the positives of fixing it up to sell."

"Maybe we do this one for you. If we like doing it, we can put money into another repair job and plan on resale." Xan wiped his face with the napkin before placing it on his plate and pushing it to the side of the table.

"So, we're doing this?" My heart pounded and my knee bounced in excitement.

"Sounds like it. When can you bring it to the shop?" Xan reached for his wallet and put his card on his bill.

I followed suit. "Bode said he'd drive me to pick up the bike tomorrow. Can I bring it by then?"

"Perfect. We'll do a diagnostic assessment tomorrow and make a plan for parts, cost, and timeline."

Once we'd paid, Xan and I walked out the front door.

"So, you must really love motorcycles. More than fry sauce? That's impressive," I teased.

"I *do* love motorcycles more than fry sauce. But only by a fraction. Please don't ever make me choose between the two." Xan clutched a hand to his chest before bumping his hip against mine as we walked down the sidewalk.

"I guess I know the way to your heart," I said. And then I realized what I'd said. "I mean, if I ever need to blackmail you or something."

We'd come to a stop because I needed to head back to my place and he needed to head toward his. Xan stared at me for a moment before blinking a few times and working his neck and shoulders in a stretch. "Yeah, either of them would be the perfect persuasion to get me to do your bidding."

I laughed. "Good to know. Maybe I should have Sage bottle up some sauce for me. Just as a precaution."

We said slightly awkward goodbyes after agreeing to touch base the next day once I knew what time Bode and I would be back in town with the bike.

* * *

The next morning, after I'd gone to visit Ginny, Bode and I headed to the far west side of Indianapolis to pick up the motorcycle.

"I hate that Ginny's having a bad few days," Bode commented as we headed back toward the city with my junked prize loaded in the back of his truck.

"It kills me to see her in pain. It was hard enough seeing her older, but the pain part is the hardest." My brow wrinkled as I thought of the pain and fatigue evident on Ginny's face as she attempted to eat a light breakfast with me at the cafeteria.

"If it helps, we've seen her go through a few rounds of pain and feeling bad since we've had Rosie." Bode offered a sympathetic smile. "It usually lasts a week or less and she bounces back. I know she's ill, but she's strong and determined. I'm not trying to offer false hope; Ginny has been adamant that we not cling to false hope or give Rosie unrealistic expectations. I'm just saying, if she's able, she'll be back to herself in no time."

I nodded and blinked away tears. "She told me pretty much the same thing this morning." I took a deep breath and blew it out slowly. "I think I'm just having a hard time because I know there's going to come a time when she doesn't bounce back, when the bouts of pain will last longer and longer until there's no break between them and she can't fight it."

Bode nodded.

We were silent for a few moments until I brought up Rosie and Oliver. We spent the rest of the drive laughing about my adorably cute sister and the equally cute Oliver and the things they said, what they did at school, and the unexpected joys—and frustrations—of parenting. I'd never really thought of having kids, but being around and helping out with Rosie and Oliver gave me some true insight into what it was like. I wasn't for or against kids at the current time, but I appreciated having the experience. And getting to know and spend time with my sister meant the world to me.

We pulled up to Whitfield's and Bode backed the truck into the drive.

Xan walked out of the shop door with a huge smile on his face.

I couldn't fight the butterflies in my stomach.

"Whoa, that's the look of a man very happy to see you," Bode murmured.

My hand froze on the door handle. "He's just excited about the bike."

Bode snorted. "Okay, if you say so."

We climbed from the truck. Bode dropped the tailgate and Xan hopped up in the truck bed. I undid the ties and helped them unload the bike.

Xan said goodbye to Bode and told me to meet him inside.

I went to the truck and gathered up my phone and hoodie as Bode climbed in.

"Be safe, don't do anything I wouldn't do," Bode teased with a wink.

My face caught fire, I murmured something that *may* have resembled a goodbye, and slammed the door.

* * *

"Holy shit, will we finish this rebuild and repair in less than five years?" I ran my eyes over the list of parts and steps Xan had jotted down. "Even if I had the money to buy all of these parts today, it looks like a very long process."

We were in the shop, a handful of employees working on bikes in the surrounding bays, but Xan had claimed a far corner workspace for our project so we weren't bothered too much by the other guys.

Xan laughed. "First, I can't say enough what a deal you

got on this beauty. She's in great shape structurally. The parts needed are standard. It may take us a while, but the rebuilding process is the fun part." He made notes on the paper. "So, we're going to charge the existing battery so we can start her up and see how she runs. We'll get a new battery to install for the final product. Carburetor rebuild will be first thing we do. Check the gas tank for rust, get that cleaned up, and then replace spark plugs. We can get those things done within a couple of work sessions. I'll order everything we need, put it on the shop's order, and then you can pay for each part as we get to it." Xan glanced at me. "If you're okay with that? Ordering on the shop's account gets a discount."

I nodded. "Yeah, as long as Bay's okay with that and it doesn't cause you any problems."

"It's all good. We'll replace all the lightbulbs and do an oil change next. Then we'll need to work on the chain and sprockets. That will take a couple sessions. Brakes will be one to two evenings of work. Tires will go on quickly." Xan clapped his hands and rubbed them together. "Then the fun stuff with custom work and detailing."

I smiled. "Is it possible you're more excited about my new bike than I am?"

Xan looked sheepish. "What? I adore fixing up motorcycles, I get to help a new friend learn how to do it, *and* we can ride together when she's all restored? What's not to be excited about?" He frowned momentarily. "Is your knee okay with riding?"

I nodded. "Yeah, it's fine. May cause some stiffness, but that's all." I rubbed my hands together. "So, when can we expect to take that first ride?"

"Well, this is a perfect time to rebuild a bike since

we're in fall and heading into winter." Xan ran his eyes over the bike. "I say we shoot for the first day of spring, but I think we'll have it done long before then."

"As long as I keep working and raking in the tips."

"Yeah, some of the items on the list will get a little pricey, but I'll get the best pieces for the lowest prices and we'll go from there." Xan slapped me on the shoulder. "Since you're getting the best of the best in labor for free, you can focus on just saving money for the parts."

His hand stayed on my shoulder and warmed the skin under my shirt. Without thinking, or maybe because I simply wanted to feel a connection, I brought my hand to my shoulder and placed it on top of his. "Awww, so humble." As if it had a mind of its own, my hand curled slightly around Xan's.

If I wasn't shocked enough at my own actions, I nearly swallowed my tongue when Xan's thumb rubbed softly against my own. The movement was brief, the touch only a moment, but the heat that traveled through my body with just that slight voluntary contact was enough to boil my blood.

I coughed and jerked my hand away. "So, you'll order things soon? Can we do anything today?"

Xan pulled his hand back, a slightly dazed expression on his face as he refocused his attention on the motorcycle. He cleared his throat. "Um, yeah. Let's get the battery out, clean it up, set it to charge. Next time we work on it, we can put the battery back in, start her up, and diagnose problems from there."

We spent the next fifteen minutes with Xan showing me how to unhook the battery.

"It's easiest and best for you to learn—and take

ownership in the work—if you do as much of this as you can on your own," he said. "But I'll be here to show you what to do and assist."

Once the battery was cleaned up, Xan demonstrated how to hook it up to the charger. He wiped his hands on his pants. "Done and done. At least for today." He paused and caught the corner of his lip between his teeth. "You, um, got plans?"

I shook my head. "You?"

"You want to try to cook something? Play some games?" Xan gestured toward the stairs that led to his apartment.

I nodded. "Sounds good."

After we cleaned up the work area, Xan went to the sink and washed his hands, and I followed. "I have the fixings for spaghetti if we want to fix that."

We said a few goodbyes and headed up the stairs.

"So, spaghetti?" Xan asked as we entered his apartment.

"Can't be too hard, right? Boil some noodles, heat some sauce?"

"I got garlic rolls and a salad too."

My heart raced that Xan had bought groceries that appeared to be planned around cooking and eating a meal with me.

For as much as we fumbled and bumbled with pots and pans, noodles and sauce, foil and greasy rolls, Xan and I moved very smoothly around each other. Our awkwardness was with the cooking more so than with each other.

When the water boiled, Xan poured the noodles into

the pot. I poured the sauce into a small pan and set it on the stove to cook.

"Next time, if we survive this meal, we should attempt homemade sauce," I suggested as I scanned the directions on the rolls for a temperature.

"Homemade sauce is the bomb. Bay brought me lasagna leftovers one day. Kyson had used Bay's grandmother Millie's recipe and the sauce was amazing."

I slid the rolls into the oven. "Ginny always says that homemade sauce makes all the difference. She used to tell my mom that. But my mom wouldn't even bother with sauce from a jar. If I wanted spaghetti it was probably coming from a can." I shivered. "Hated that slimy stuff."

Xan's eyes grew wide. "Shit, do you not like spaghetti?"

"No, I like actual spaghetti, not that canned shit."

"Speaking of Ginny, how's she doing?"

My mouth pulled down at the corners and an immediate sting of tears filled my eyes. "She's had a few rough days. Bode was trying to reassure me that she's had quite a few rounds of rough days, but she always bounces back." I took a deep breath and appreciated that Xan was listening, simply waiting quietly for me to continue. "I think I'm mostly fearful of the day, whenever it comes, where she doesn't bounce back. She has cancer and it's not going away; she knows that and has made sure we all know it. But she's determined to stay around for as long as possible." A breath shuddered from me. "It's just scary and sad to know that a day will come when her determination is no longer stronger than the disease that's killing her. It's bad enough I'm going to lose her, but knowing Rosie will lose the closest thing to a real mom she's ever had is eating me up inside."

Xan's hand tugged on my shoulder until I turned to face him and my breathing ceased to function as he pulled me close, his arms wrapped around my middle. "I'm sorry. It seems unfair that you just got her back and now you're facing losing her again."

I allowed my arms to reach around Xan's shoulders and I held on tightly as a barrage of emotions and tears spilled from me. Burying my face in Xan's neck as I cried, I let him hold me and attempted to push away the embarrassment of crying in his arms.

As the tears subsided, I found myself plastered to Xan's warm strength, holding onto his support, and fighting the urge to nuzzle against the skin of his neck. I froze when Xan's chin rubbed against the side of my head. An inch lower and his mouth would be just a whisper from my ear, his lips so close to touching my skin.

And then I smelled smoke and something scorched. I jerked away from Xan to find thin wisps of smoke coming from the oven. Quickly, I turned off the oven and pulled the rolls out. They were no longer recognizable as bread, just small chunks of charcoal.

"Open some windows," I commanded and turned on the oven exhaust. So far, the smoke detector hadn't gone off, but I wasn't sure we had avoided it completely.

The lid of the saucepan rattled. After realizing the handle was much too hot, I grabbed the pan from the burner and sat it in the sink before removing the lid. I found a sizzling, congealed blob of sauce which appeared to have burned along the bottom of the pan.

"Fuck," I mumbled.

"Um, I don't think the noodles are supposed to look like this," Xan said from his place in front of the stove. "What the hell happened? How the fuck did we screw up this bad?"

I ran a hand over my face. "Well, for my part, I meant to turn the sauce down to low and forgot." I picked up the roll package and read it again. "And I should have paid more attention because this said to preheat to four-fifty and then *turn it down* to three-twenty-five. I missed that part."

"So, what's my excuse?" Xan frowned. "Water, boil, cook the noodles."

I glanced in the pot. "Maybe more water? Maybe we let it boil away too much and cooked the noodles too long?"

"Well, shit. This is a disaster." Xan chuckled.

"Not completely," I assured. "We messed up the food, but nothing actually burned down, no fire department had to be called, and I don't think this pan is ruined. Nothing a good scrubbing can't fix."

"Well, what do we do now? I don't want a damn salad by itself for dinner." Xan crossed his arms over his chest.

"Order take out from The Salty Lizard and eat our salad with dinner?" I raised a brow.

Xan smiled slightly. "I'm on board with that. And then we play Mortal Kombat so I can kick your ass."

"Or we play Mortal Kombat so *I* can kick *your* ass." I elbowed him.

Xan pulled out his phone. "We'll see."

Our moment had been interrupted by the burned food. Was it even a moment? Maybe it was just Xan offering comfort because he knew I was upset about my aunt.

Maybe I made it weird by feeling more than I should have when he had me wrapped in his arms.

Yeah, I'd definitely read too much into it and needed to push the feelings away. We were just two friends eating dinner and playing games. Nothing more.

* * *

"Hey man, I'm sorry if I made you uncomfortable earlier," Bode's words were quiet as he left Oliver's room after putting the child to bed.

I'd read a story to both kids, tucked Rosie in with hugs and kisses, and then flopped down on the couch to wait for Bode. He'd said he wanted to talk to me, but I wasn't sure about what.

My face wrinkled in confusion.

"I told Sage about how I was teasing you when I dropped you at the shop. Telling you to be safe and not do anything I wouldn't do." Bode grimaced. "Sage pointed out that I may have made you uncomfortable and I want to apologize. It wasn't my intention, but I'm sorry for saying anything at all."

My face heated and I sighed before running a hand through my short hair. "It was maybe a bit embarrassing, but I wasn't uncomfortable." I paused. I knew I should probably keep my mouth shut, but Bode was right there and maybe he could help me put things in perspective. "The only thing that's uncomfortable is whatever's between me and Xan."

Bode's brows shot up and he waited.

"I like him. As a friend, obviously, but as more than that too. But I feel like I need to get over the feelings because we're just friends and he doesn't feel the same." The words poured from me like spring water from a burbling brook.

Bode smiled and took a seat. "Okay, first, you've got to be blind to not see how Xan looks at you."

I bit my lip. "Really?"

"Yeah, really." Bode nodded. "Have you ever dated a guy?"

I shook my head.

"Been with a guy?"

I shook my head.

"Kissed a guy?"

Another head shake.

"Been attracted to a guy?"

I nodded. "Yeah, I've found men attractive ever since I hit puberty. Just never gave it much thought—that's pretty easy when you're busy trying to stay alive with a neglectful and abusive parent. I dated some girls, had sex with them, but dating was hard in the Army and I'm not one for a lot of random hookups."

"Okay, that's all fine. There's not a specific timeline or special requirements. Even if you'd never found men attractive, it would be completely okay for you to find Xan attractive now." Bode shifted on the couch. "So, I'm thinking you and Xan should talk about it, see if you're on the same page."

My eyes nearly bugged out of my head. "How do you propose I do that? 'So, hey, I know we just became friends and all that, but I think you're hella hot and I kinda want to kiss you and a bunch of other shit.' I don't see that going over well."

Bode chuckled. "You never know, maybe he's thinking the same thing and would be glad you brought it up."

I took a deep breath and blew it out harshly. "This is so crazy. What if I bring it up and he's feeling the same? I've never done anything with a guy, what would we even do?" I leaned forward and rested my head in my hands.

"You've kissed girls? Had sex with them? Various other sexual acts?" Bode's words were patient.

I nodded.

"Kissing is exactly the same. Start there."

"But there's more and I'm clueless." I groaned.

"Hand jobs are great. You touch him the same way you know feels good. Blow jobs don't have to happen, but if you're both on board, they are amazing. You suck him just like you know feels good on you."

"Oh my God, is this what it's like when a kid hits puberty and has the sex talk with a parent? I'm dying." My face was on fire and I couldn't look up from my shoes.

Bode laughed loudly and clapped a hand over his mouth as if afraid he'd wake the kids. "I'm not sure most of those first sex talks are about mutual oral sex, but what do I know?" Bode's face froze in a mask of terror. "Oh my God, am I going to have to have sex talks with Oliver and Rosie?"

I snorted. "Probably. Maybe skip the detailed instructions the first time around."

We sat silently for a few moments.

"I'm pretty sure I should be offended that I've been pigeon-holed into the parent role here. I'm not *that* much older than you." Bode frowned as he teased. "There's a lot more you can do together. Rub off through your clothes, rub off together with no clothes, simultaneous blow jobs in the sixty-nine position, rimming, anal, and about a million other things. A couple has to experiment and see what they both find feels good." He paused and looked as if he was thinking hard about something. "I gotta say, I think some good old-fashioned gay porn would be extremely beneficial in this situation. If you both find that you're on the same page as far as feelings."

"Gay porn? I'm in," Sage whispered with a huge smile as he came into the living room. "Seriously, why are you talking about porn? Aren't we like a family-friendly establishment these days?"

"Father Bode is giving me the birds and the bees talk because I may have admitted I really like Xan and have no clue about sex with a man," I summarized the conversation with a wave of my hand.

Sage chuckled. "I love it. Do you have any questions? Bode and I can answer anything or help you find the answer. If you're interested in toys—a butt plug can help stretch your ass if you decide to do anal—I can help with that."

Bode snorted. "So can Bay's grandmother, Millie."

Sage buried his head on Bode's shoulder. "Oh my God, she probably could."

I raised a brow. "Do I even want to know?"

"Millie bought Bay and Kyson a dildo and told a very entertaining story about that and some other purchases," Bode explained through his laughter.

"Okay, I think I'll start with questions to the both of you and porn, but if I need a dildo, I'll consider Millie." As weird as the conversation had gotten, my heart was warm to know I was supported by friends.

"And be sure to talk to Xan. I'm pretty sure you and he

are having the same feelings, but being open and honest is the best plan." Sage spoke to me but leaned up to nuzzle the side of Bode's neck. "Unless he's like this big doofus who spent a *very* long time trying to convince himself, me, and everyone else that he wasn't interested in me."

Bode kissed the top of Sage's head. "I learned my lesson. But, for real, just talk to Xan."

"What if he's not feeling the same and it messes up our friendship?" My stomach hurt just thinking about it.

"What if he's feeling the same and you find the love of a lifetime?" Sage countered.

"I need the love of a friend, not necessarily a romantic love," I argued.

"Nothing says they can't be one and the same," Bode added as he took Sage's hand.

"Maybe you two will find a love you never knew you were missing," Sage offered. "Would be a shame to miss out on an epic love out of fear."

My cheeks puffed with a breath I held until I began to feel lightheaded. "Thanks. You've given me a lot to think about."

"Oh, we've given you more than that," Bode stated.

I frowned.

"I'll give you my account information for the top three porn sites. It's a gift that keeps on giving," Bode teased.

We all laughed.

# 14

---

## XAN

DINNER WITH CHASE and working on his bike were easily my favorite parts of the day. I spent all day doing what I absolutely adored—what I felt I was born to do—and then the evenings and weekends hanging out with Chase and fixing up his bike.

But hanging out with Chase had quickly become the most dreaded part of my days as well. I had no clue what to do with the feelings I was having toward him. If it had just been a physical attraction, maybe I could have pushed it aside, jacked off until the desire and longing passed, or maybe thought about a hookup or a date.

*If* the attraction had been only physical.

It wasn't. It most definitely wasn't.

I liked Chase. Enjoyed talking to him, adored laughing and joking with him, just loved being around him. And that was the problem. I didn't know how to deal with an emotional and physical attraction to my best friend.

Hell, up until recently, I had never in my life had a best friend.

And now I wanted to spend all my time with him, tell him what he meant to me, touch him, kiss him. And *more*.

I sighed as I waited for Chase to arrive at the shop for a work session with his beauty.

"What's up?" Bay asked as he wiped his hands on a towel after helping someone at one of the front bays.

"Just waiting on Chase. We're using his old battery for now and got the carburetor rebuilt last time. Planning on cleaning the gas tank and replacing sparkplugs today." I ran a cloth over the bike. It wasn't in top physical condition just yet, but it was going to be stunning when it was done. "Chase seems to be enjoying the work and learning the ins and outs."

Bay smiled slyly. "Sounds good. But my 'what's up?' was more a 'what's bothering you?'"

I began to protest and deny anything Bay may have been hinting at. But I glanced around the shop, noticed there were only a couple people working. Both Cliff and Eve had their earbuds in and were in their own little worlds as they tinkered around on their projects.

I took a deep breath, chewed on my lip for a moment, and then whispered, "If I tell you something, can you promise not to tell anyone else?"

Bay chuckled. "Well, if it's about you and Chase being hot for each other, I've gotta tell you that most everyone knows that already."

My mouth gaped open and I stared at Bay for several moments. Rather than arguing with him, I shrugged. "Okay, so what do I do about it?"

"Have you talked to Chase?"

"Kinda a hard thing to bring up to someone who has just recently become your best friend. What if it fucks things up between us?" I propped both hands on my hips.

"What if it doesn't?" Bay winked.

I huffed.

"You find him attractive. You like spending time with him. You guys get along great. Why not address the situation head-on, be honest, and see where things go?" Bay crossed his arms over his chest. "I'm speaking from personal experience; avoiding and hiding and pretending the feelings aren't there only makes things worse."

"So, I just hand him a wrench, walk him through installing the new plugs, and casually bring up the fact that I like him, between telling him to lube the spark plug boot and button it up?" I rolled my eyes. "Great plan. Sure it will go over well."

Bay laughed. "Maybe bringing up lubing the boot and buttoning it up will open a conversation?"

I groaned.

"Just pick a time when you're both relaxed, you have time for a real conversation, and some privacy in case it goes the way I think you're both hoping it will go." Bay slapped me on the back. "I've seen the way you two look at each other and the smiles on your faces whenever the other is around. Give it a shot, take a chance. I think it will work out for the best."

\* \* \*

About two hours later, Chase and I were cleaning up from our work on the motorcycle.

"Pizza, beer, and Mortal Kombat?" I asked.

"Definitely." Chase tossed a shop towel in a basket and

stretched his arms over his head. The glimpse I got of pale, smooth skin and a light smattering of hair around his navel had me staring and I had to force myself to look away. "Today was kinda a bitch at work."

"Come on, let's wash up and you can tell me about it." I gestured toward the stairs.

Chase froze and stared at me for a beat before his face softened. "Sorry, just weird to realize I have someone to shoot the shit with about good or bad days. I know Ginny wants to hear about my life, but I saw her this morning and about an hour visit was all she could handle."

We headed up the stairs, me wondering the whole time if Chase would be staring at my ass as much as I wanted to be ogling his.

I pulled out the heavy-duty soap and turned on the kitchen sink. "Scrub-a-dub-dub."

"So, now I'm your man-in-the-tub?" Chase elbowed me.

I laughed. "Nursery rhymes are kinda weird. I don't remember many of them. It's not like my mom or dad were reading to me as a little kid." I scrubbed at my knuckles. "I had one foster mom who read to us, but there were so many damn kids that it was hard to pay attention. I remember a teacher teaching us nursery rhymes and using them to help us learn to read. Probably in Kindergarten or first grade?" I handed the bar of soap to Chase. "Tell me about your day."

Chase took the soap and lathered his hands. "Nothing hugely terrible, just kinda off all day. Like I was distracted I guess, and I messed up an order. Other than that, it felt like a lot of the customers were bitchy or maybe I was just grumpy." He scrubbed under his nails. "Maybe it was just one of those days. Sage and Bode seemed to be rubbing each other wrong, too."

We rinsed and dried our hands, our wet skin slick as we inadvertently touched.

"They seem like an amazing couple and great dads," I began, "but I'm sure they fight like all relationships."

"Mostly they bicker, I've not seen a full-on argument. Honestly, I think Bode does everything he can to keep Sage happy. But they are really a good match as far as personalities and sense of humor." Chase pulled out his phone. "I'll order pizza. Want a large with everything?"

"Extra-large with everything minus the black olives." I grabbed two beers from the fridge. "We can play until the pizza gets here."

We flopped on the couch and were soon immersed in a competitive game of Mortal Kombat.

"You see Bay and his husband together much?" Chase asked.

"Yeah, Kyson comes to the shop sometimes. I've hung out at their place a few times. They seem to be just as great of a couple and dads as Sage and Bode. Their kids are super cute. Arlo loves Legos. Cori is too little for much but she likes to be held and the guys say she's starting to get into everything." I kept my eyes on the screen as I spoke.

"You have a lot of gay friends growing up?" Chase asked and my heart froze. He was probably just making small-talk. Just because *I* was considering bringing up my attraction didn't mean he was planning the same.

"When I was little, it wasn't something I even thought of. Friends in school were simply friends and I never got to hang around any one place long enough to learn more than just their names. By the time I reached puberty and maybe would have started recognizing my own sexuality or that of others, I was in too deep with the club. And *no way* a gay person, or even a bisexual person, would have survived coming out in that situation." I paused the game for a moment. "I told Bay this, but figure I should tell you too. The clubs I was with kinda pimped me out to any women willing to pay with cash or drugs or favors. I realized much later that what they were doing was wrong, but as a horny and well-developed teen, I thought it was great." I turned back to the game. "I had a feeling there were some males who would have paid for a turn with me, but none ever dared to attempt it."

"I'm really sorry that happened to you." He leaned into my shoulder for a too-brief moment. "So, um, are you gay?" Chase's words were soft next to me.

I was silent for a moment.

"Sorry, that was rude, you don't have to answer that," he mumbled.

"No, it's okay. I think I'm definitely bisexual. I enjoyed sex with women. Maybe more so back then than now." I scoffed. "Not that I've been having much sex lately. The few women I tried to date or hookup with have just felt wrong and annoying. I'm sure that's more on me than on them." I gritted my teeth and took a breath. "What about you?"

Chase took his turn to pause the game. "A year ago, I would have said no. But, now, I'm not so sure. It's like I got a new chance at life and finally got to relax and have some stability, and now all these thoughts and feelings and questions are bombarding me."

I felt his eyes on me. I nodded, but inwardly breathed a sigh of relief when he went back to playing the game.

"I've realized a lot about myself recently. One of the biggest things being that I've found several guys attractive in the past. I'd always just shoved it away—I guess trying to make it on my own and not be pulled under by my mom was a bigger distraction than even I realized."

We played the game silently for several moments until the door buzzed.

We both startled. I stood and gulped the rest of my beer before heading to the door.

Behind me, Chase paused the game and followed.

By the time we returned to the living room, we had pizza, napkins, and two new beers each.

I turned the TV to a random movie as we ate.

When only a couple pieces of pizza remained, we both popped open a third beer.

"So, this is maybe going to be weird," Chase blurted just as I opened my mouth and started to say, "So, I wanted to talk to you about something."

Chase bit his lip and his gorgeous pale skin flushed pink at the same time my face flamed hot.

"You go ahead," Chase offered.

I took a deep breath. "I am really glad we've become friends and I'd like to hang onto that."

Chase nodded as if he agreed, but his mouth turned down at the corners. "I want that too."

"But," I started.

"But?" Chase frowned. "Buts are never good, right?"

I smiled a bit. "I'm hoping in this case the but is good."

Chase's brows shot up.

"Shit, that came out wrong." I laughed and ran a hand over my face. "Actually, it may have come out just right," I hedged.

"Are we talking *but* or *butt*?" Chase narrowed his eyes.

"Shit, this is even harder than I imagined it would be." I took a long swallow of beer. "I like you. Like, I *like* you. Fuck, why do I feel like I'm back in grade school where kids were passing notes with a check yes or no box?" I took a deep breath. "I find you insanely attractive. I love spending time with you. And I was wondering…"

Chase covered the space between us in a nanosecond and his mouth captured mine mid-sentence. The kiss was unpracticed and awkward as fuck, but it was also the most sincere and intense kiss of my life. Just as my tongue began to coax his mouth open, Chase groaned and froze.

He jerked away with a gasp. "I'm so sorry. I shouldn't have done that." He stood as if to leave.

I stood and took his hand. "Nuh-uh, no way. You can't kiss me like that, give me only the slightest taste, and then act like it was a mistake. You're not walking away just yet."

Chase brushed fingers tentatively over his lips as his gaze traveled between my lips and my eyes. "I shouldn't have interrupted. I shouldn't have assumed you wanted that."

After moving both of his hands to rest on my shoulders, I cupped his face. "I very much wanted that. What I was stumbling around trying to say was that I like you and wanted to see how you felt about me."

Chase closed his eyes and pressed his cheek against my hand. "I like you. I can't stop thinking about you. I love every second we spend together. You're my best friend, and I'm scared to lose that, but I definitely feel the same way you're feeling." He pursed his lips. "I mean, I guess I'm feeling the same."

"Do you want to touch me and kiss me, spend time with me, and see what could happen if we took things to the next level of this friendship?" I asked as my thumb caressed his cheek.

Chase nodded.

"Any buts?" I teased.

"Just worried that we'll mess this up. What if one of us wants it more than the other? What if we start something and realize it's not going to work? Where does that leave us?" Chase bit the inside corner of his lip.

As my thumb moved to trail over his lips, the lips I longed to kiss, I caught his eye. "I think we keep communication open and honest. If one of us realizes we aren't feeling it, we respect each other enough to maturely accept that it wasn't meant to be, and we go back to being friends." My fingers itched to grip his face and devour his mouth. "We could start with a kiss and see if we're both on the same page?"

Chase licked his lips and nodded.

As much as I'd always cherish that impulsive, sloppy first kiss, I wanted nothing more than to savor every second of each new kiss we shared from that moment on. And if this was to be the only kiss before Chase decided swapping spit with me wasn't his thing, I planned to enjoy it.

I closed the gap between us, my mouth hovering over his for a moment as I took in his scent, his warmth, his increased breathing. Slowly, almost as if I was afraid I'd scare him away if I moved too quickly, I dipped my head and brushed my lips against his.

The catch in Chase's breathing did me in and I deepened the kiss. Our lips glided and pressed before Chase's tongue darted out to tease at my bottom lip. When he retreated, I gave chase and followed his tongue into his mouth. He tasted of beer and pizza and just *Chase*.

When he groaned and snaked his arms around my neck, I wrapped my arms around his waist and pulled him close. The instant our jean-clad erections brushed, an electric jolt of desire shot through me and I knew I was definitely onboard with seeing if this could lead anywhere.

But I pulled back to check on Chase. Pressing my forehead against his, I caught my breath. "You okay?"

Chase nodded with a chuckle. "Yeah, kinda a lot better than okay. What do you think? On the same page?"

"Oh, hell yeah," I murmured before capturing his mouth again and pulling him down to the couch. With my legs spread and my back against the arm of the sofa, Chase fit perfectly against me and nestled his hips against mine as the kiss continued.

He pulled away a few moments later, panting. "I want to do more, but I don't know how much is too much right now?"

My hands trailed down his back and grasped his ass. "I'd love to see you naked and touch you. Maybe nothing beyond hand jobs and making out tonight?"

Chase nodded eagerly. "Have you ever watched porn? Like gay porn?"

The question caught me off-guard and I laughed. "A few times. Why?"

Chase shrugged through his pink cheeks. "Bode

suggested I could watch some and ask him and Sage if I had questions. I just wondered if you'd watched it and what you thought." He rocked his hips against mine.

"Wait, first question, did you talk to Bode about us?" I raised a brow.

Chase winced and nodded. "Yeah, I'm sorry. He and Sage have been saying there's something between us, and I finally broke down and admitted I liked you and had no clue how to handle it."

I chuckled. "No worries. I only asked because I talked to Bay about us. Kinda the same thing. He's been telling me over and over that it's evident we like each other. He told me we should just talk." I brushed a soft kiss against his lips. "This is so fucking amazing. I've wanted to kiss you and touch you for so long, and now you're right here."

Chase returned the kiss. "So, thoughts on porn?"

I cleared my throat. "I've seen enough to know a lot of it's not realistic, but it's hot and could probably give us some ideas of things we'd like to try." I moved my hands to the top of his waistband and teased my fingers under the material.

"Maybe we watch some before next time and come armed with things we'd like to try?" Chase raised his brow.

"Sounds perfect." My finger played at the cleft of his ass. "Now, I'd love to get back to naked and touching. You game?"

Chase smiled and nodded before kissing me again as he rolled his cock against mine.

But too soon, he froze.

My heart plummeted. Was he changing his mind?

"What's wrong?" I placed my hand against his cheek.

"I want to do sexual stuff with you, definitely." He rocked his hips slightly. "But I'm not interested in *only* sex. If sex is all you want, I need to know before I let my heart get involved in this."

My hand moved to the back of his head. "Too late, my heart is already involved." I pulled him forward and kissed him until his mouth opened and accepted my tongue.

He groaned. "Good to know," he murmured against my lips before diving back into the kiss.

As much as I wanted to strip us both naked and run my tongue over every inch of his body, I didn't want to rush things. "You want to do this here or in bed?"

Chase pressed his hot body against me with a slight moan. "Here sounds great," he pressed kisses along my jaw, "but the bed would allow us more room."

"Bed. Now." I pushed up from the couch.

Chase followed me to the bed. "I want to undress you, is that okay?" His cheeks pinked adorably.

I nodded, unable to breathe.

He slowly lifted my shirt over my head.

I gasped as he placed his warm hands over my chest and slid them over my nipples. The reverent look on his face as his hands trailed over my abs and down to the waistband of my jeans made my heart flutter.

Chase licked his lips as he undid the button and pushed my jeans down. My dick strained against the black boxer briefs and I hissed when Chase ran a hand over my hot cock.

With nostrils flaring, Chase stroked me through the fabric with his eyes locked on mine.

"My turn," I growled.

I yanked his shirt over his head and sighed when my eyes took in his gorgeous pale skin, light hair, and dusky nipples. I'd seen him shirtless before, but the anticipation of what was next had me nearly panting.

I teased his nipples and was rewarded with a breathy moan before I hooked my thumbs in his beltloops and pulled him closer. I unbuttoned his jeans and worked them over his fine ass before pushing them to his knees.

His cocked pressed against light grey briefs and the wet spot I saw had me ready to drop to my knees and swallow him to the root. Instead, since we were treading softly for now, I stroked a finger along his erection and traced my thumb over the wet spot.

As if by unspoken agreement, we shucked our pants all the way off and tumbled onto the bed. After rolling around, tongues teasing and thrusting, hips rocking, cocks rubbing, we eventually ended up with Chase flat on his back, legs spread, and me pressed perfectly against him.

I played with the waist of his briefs. When our eyes met, I raised my brow in question. Chase nodded and I smiled slyly. Teasing my thumb under the elastic, I tugged until the material began to shift.

Chase lifted his ass and shimmied to assist in removing the underwear.

His cock was gorgeous. Thick and cut, leaking precum, and begging to be touched.

I shifted to my knees and pulled my boxers off.

Chase's nostrils flared and he bit his lip when my dick sprang loose and slapped my belly.

I stroked myself once, twice, while never taking my eyes from Chase before taking my place back between his legs. Our lips met as our cocks pressed together between us and we both groaned at the delicious friction.

"Fuck, that feels amazing," Chase murmured against my lips.

"So good," I agreed.

"Gotta be honest, not going to last very long if you keep rubbing against me like that." Chase threw his head back as I rocked into him hard and kissed his neck.

"Same," I panted.

"Wait, I want to touch you before it's over." Chase snaked his hand between us and took my length in his warm hand.

"Fuuuck," I cried out. "Really won't last with you doing that."

I shifted to my side next to Chase and took his cock in my fist.

Chase whimpered.

We stroked each other, our throbbing cocks leaking and begging for release.

I ran my thumb over Chase's slit and he shuddered. "Next time, I want to taste you," I whispered as I released him and rolled back between his legs.

"Fuck, yes." Chase groaned as I began rutting against him. "Oh God, that's so good. Gonna come."

"Wanna watch you come, feel you paint my skin." I thrust my hips hard and slow before taking both our cocks in my fist and stroking.

Chase placed his hand over mine.

My balls drew up tight just as Chase growled. Our hot cum spilled over our fingers as we both groaned, our cocks throbbing in our fists.

We lay motionless, only our chests heaving as we caught our breath.

"That was amazing," Chase whispered. "Yeah?"

"Definitely," I agreed. My heart soared to hear we seemed to be totally on board with this whole *us* thing.

"We're sticky," Chase mumbled against my shoulder.

I grabbed a towel I'd hung on the bedpost and wiped my hand, stomach, and cock before handing the cloth to Chase.

Once he was cleaned up, I flopped down on the bed and opened my arm.

Chase's face broke into a beautiful smile and he snuggled into my arms, his back to my chest.

We fell to sleep almost immediately.

# 15

CHASE

I'D BEEN WALKING on air ever since Xan and I talked and took things to the next level. In a way, I was kicking myself for taking so long to see what others had seen and just talk to Xan about it. But, on the other hand, I felt it was probably for the best that we'd had time to build our friendship first. It was so strange—but amazing—how easy it was for the two of us to talk and make that move from friends to more.

Sex with Xan had been the best sexual experience I'd ever had. Waking up in his arms was even better. And continuing to spend time together, having dinner and rebuilding my bike, was absolutely perfect. After years of being on edge about my mom, feeling alone even while part of a group in the Army, having a friend—actually, having multiple friends I could turn to—and being able to just relax, settle in somewhere I felt welcome, and enjoy life was kinda overwhelming. But it was the best type of overwhelming I'd ever felt.

My mind went back to the evening in Xan's apartment.

*After we napped a bit, I woke and shifted my ass against Xan's cock enough until he awakened and growled as his stiff length pressed along my ass.*

*"You looking for a second round?" Xan growled.*

*I rolled in his arms and reached for his cock as I captured his mouth in a slow, exploratory kiss. Xan groaned and extended his hand to fist my dick. With our tongues dancing, our hands stroked a rhythm until we both erupted.*

*After a relaxing shower with roaming hands and slow kisses, we dressed and wandered to the door.*

*"So, Plan Porn is in place for the next date?" I teased.*

*Xan chuckled. "I'm down. Bring at least one thing you want to try."*

*"Perfect." I bit my lip. "I'll have to thank Bode and Sage for sharing their accounts."*

*"Friends who share premium account passwords are worth keeping." Xan winked and kissed me. "I'm really glad we decided to do this."*

*I'd leaned into him and whispered, "Me too. This was amazing. I haven't been focused on intimacy or a relationship for most of my life, so having the chance to take this step with my best friend is really kinda great."*

*"Fucking great," Xan murmured against my mouth before kissing me soft and slow. "I've never had a best friend, never been involved with a friend, never been involved with a man, so all of this is going to be new to me. I'm sure I'll fuck it up somehow."*

*"Hey." I placed my hand against his cheek. "This is all new to me, too. We'll be patient with each other and fuck up together."*

*Xan smiled and nodded. "Sounds like a good plan." He kissed me soundly. "Thank you for a great evening."*

I'd left and floated home with a smile that I hadn't been able to wipe away. Hadn't *wanted* to wipe away. I was happy and content. Not fearful, not anxious, not alone. For the first time in my life, my future looked sunny, the glass was half-full, I had people on my side, and I was looking forward to what came next.

* * *

Ginny's color and energy were back to normal and she was chomping at the bit to get out, visit Rosie, see her friends, and "blow the stink off me" as she put it.

We headed to The Salty Lizard. Ginny was meeting up with Bay's mom and grandmother. They planned to walk Mass. Ave. to see the shops, pay a visit to The Silver and Gold Creative to check out Rhys and Benji's art, and then come back to The Lizard for lunch. Ginny was staying until Rosie got home from school and then one of us would take her back to Rose Gardens.

Sage, Bode, and I had talked about the importance of having Rosie and Ginny together as much as possible to build happy memories. As long as Ginny was physically able, we planned on having her with us as often as we could. I wanted my sister to have great memories of her mother in the years to come. As much as I hated that Rosie would inevitably lose Ginny, I'd seen first-hand that she had been blessed with two terrific dads who loved her very much. Sage was fond of pointing out that Rosie was lucky to have her big brother around as well. I didn't feel like I was that important to her life, but I knew how glad I was to have the chance to know my sister.

By the time the main lunch rush was over, Millie,

Bonnie, and Ginny came through the door talking and laughing like the best of friends. I smiled and waved to let them know I'd be over to take care of them in a moment.

Once I had their drinks served and orders placed, Millie patted the seat next to her at their usual booth. "Sit down, dear. We have wonderful things to tell you."

My eyes went wide. Millie was a major character and I never had any idea what she was going to say. But I sat for a moment since the place was clearing out from the lunch crowd.

"We're having a party. A dinner. A dinner party, but not one of those stuffy affairs with snooty people and pretentious food and drink." Millie patted my hand. "We'll have it here at The Lizard. I've already cleared it with Bode. You can, of course, invite your new beau." She leaned in close. "He's very stunning in that tattooed bad-boy, do-all-the-dirty-things-to-me type of way."

My face caught fire.

Ginny snorted.

Bonnie groaned.

"I'm sure Chase is learning all about the fun he and Xan can have," Ginny added and winked at me.

The kitchen bell rang and I jumped up to grab the order. "A party sounds great. I'll be there. Is this open to kids?"

"Of course, we want all the kids there." Bonnie nodded.

"There will be food, drinks, desserts, music, and dancing." Millie motioned me to come closer.

I threw a desperate glance toward the kitchen, but leaned in close.

"Dancing is a great form of foreplay. Be sure to take

care of *preparations* in case you and that man of yours find yourselves in the throes of passion on the dance floor and have to high-tail it out of here to feed the fire between you." Millie smiled slyly. "I feel it's best to buy the family-size enemas. And if you've not experimented with toys, I know a place. Just ask Bode, I'm sure he'd assist. He was very helpful when I was buying for Bay and Kyson."

I choked on the air I attempted to breathe and could only nod as I coughed and wiped at my watering eyes. By the time I reached the order window to grab the food, Bode was watching me and laughing.

"I see Millie gotcha, huh?"

"That woman is something else. I'm not sure what, but definitely something else." I glanced toward the table where the women were laughing. "She told me to buy the family pack of enemas and that you could help me find toys."

Bode snorted. "Bay prefers she use the term bulk-size. And, she's not wrong about the toys. You let me know." He leaned in and whispered, "A butt plug would help a lot with stretching if you guys are thinking about anal."

"Oh my God," I hissed. "You're as bad as Millie." I elbowed him, grabbed the food, and rushed off to deliver it before I inevitably had to return to Ginny's table for more embarrassment.

By the time the ladies finished their meal and seemingly ran out of things to talk about, Rosie was rushing in the door behind Oliver.

The kids ran to the back to put their school stuff in the office and grab a snack.

Millie and Bonnie said goodbye and Ginny headed to the back to visit with Rosie.

Based on how much the women had laughed and hooted about the dinner party they were planning, I had a feeling it was going to be quite the affair.

* * *

I made sure both the doors to my room were locked before settling on the bed to open the site Sage had assured me was the best for quality porn. *That* had been an awkward conversation. Luckily, Sage didn't make me suffer for long before he wrote down the address, username, and password.

With shaking hands, I typed in the address and then Sage's login information. It wasn't as if I'd *never* seen bits and pieces of porn. I was in the Army and plenty of guys watched it, shared it, and flashed it around.

However, this was different. At least in my head. This was me purposely logging into a paid site. This was me choosing to watch two men have sex. This was me preparing for what Xan and I would maybe be doing together soon. My cock grew hard just thinking about it.

I took a few moments to peruse the layout of the site and the various category choices. My heart pounded in my chest and my dick pressed hard against my jeans. I quickly undid the button and zipper for comfort.

Having no clue what I liked as far as category or trope or kink, I settled on the video of the day. The two men were probably about twenty-five to thirty. One had dark hair, one was blond. *Holy shit*. Could it be any more like Xan and me?

As the video progressed from the men awkwardly chatting about a video game to kissing, I found myself completely hooked. The men were cute, but I was picturing Xan and me kissing, hands roaming, cocks bulging behind jeans.

Item number one on my list was going to be kissing for sure. Maybe it wasn't super sexual or kinky, but I'd had a taste of Xan's mouth and I wanted it again and again.

The men on my computer screen undressed each other while flicking and pinching nipples. I teased my own nipple under my shirt. Yeah, that felt good. Imagining Xan doing that with his teeth and tongue? Add it to the list.

By the end of the video, my cock was throbbing and leaking. The guys on the screen had jerked each other, sucked each other, rimmed each other, and fucked in all sorts of positions. The title had indicated *flip fucking* and I used my prior knowledge and what I saw to conclude that meant the men taking turns being the top.

My list was getting very, *very* long.

I pushed the laptop to the side and gripped my cock. Every stroke, I pictured Xan's hand and mouth on me and mine on his. When I thumbed my slit, I threw my head back and groaned as I imagined Xan's tongue dipping in to tease and taste.

Quickly, I shucked my jeans and underwear before grabbing some lube. I'd rolled my eyes when Bode tossed it on my bed as "a gift," but now I was grateful for the small bottle. Once my fingers and shaft were slick, I pressed a digit against my hole until the muscle gave way and allowed my finger entrance. The sting was powerful but brief, and I soon added a second finger as I stroked my cock. I closed my eyes and pictured Xan's shaft sliding into my ass and groaned. The image of my hard length thrusting in and out of Xan's body tipped me over the edge. Thick, hot ropes of cum painted my belly as I moaned and pictured Xan's cum mixed with mine.

*Holy fuck.*

When I finally caught my breath and cleaned up, I texted Xan.

**Me:** *Watched some porn. I've got a list. A very long list.*

**Xan:** *Fuck, if I wasn't with Bay and Kyson right now, I'd ask for details.*

**Me:** *Next time we're together, we get started on the list and work our way through. You game?*

**Xan:** *Fuck yeah.*

\* \* \*

By the time Xan and I finished that day's planned work on my bike, I felt as if I was going to explode if I didn't get my hands and mouth on him soon.

Xan must have felt the same because he chased me up the stairs and pressed me against the wall as soon as the door closed behind us. His mouth was on me, tongue plunging deep, hips rocking into mine, arms wrapped around me as he gripped my ass.

When we finally broke the kiss, Xan grinned and licked

his lips. "Been wanting to do that for the last two hours. Couldn't wait any longer."

"Glad you did it, I'd been wanting to do the same." I kissed him again.

"You want to eat or work on that list first?" Xan waggled his brow.

"Let's do list, then eat, then get back to the list."

"Perfect." Xan grabbed my hand and led me to his bed. "What's first?"

"Well, that," I gestured toward the door, "is top on my list. I love kissing you and I never want to stop. So, kissing is always a go-to for me."

"Noted and agreed," Xan murmured against my mouth. "Next?"

"I don't think I want anal tonight. For either of us. Not just yet. I'm down with bottoming, I just don't want to rush it." I bit my lip. "What about you?"

"In most of my fantasies, I'm topping you, but I'm not against bottoming as long as it's *you* sliding your cock deep in my ass." Xan cupped my hardening dick as he spoke. "But anal can wait. What else?"

"I definitely want blow jobs. You sucking me, me sucking you, I don't care, but I definitely want this cock in my mouth. Soon." I palmed his bulge.

Xan groaned. "God, yes. I can't stop thinking about you fucking my face, sliding your dick between my lips and pressing deep to the back of my throat while I grip your hips."

"Fuuuuck," I groaned.

"What about rimming?" Xan asked.

"I definitely want to try it. Maybe after proper

preparations and a shower? It looks amazing, but I think it's probably best when prepared."

"Agreed." Xan nuzzled my neck. "So, what do we start with tonight?"

"Blow jobs? Then after dinner we can do more?"

"But we're agreed on no anal tonight?"

I nodded.

"What about ass play, just no dicks in ass?"

"I'm on board with that." I nodded.

"Then strip and lay down. I've been dying to taste your cock and feel your lips around mine." Xan gave me a little shove.

We ended up in a naked, writhing mess of arms and legs as we kissed and touched, teased and stroked. Xan took over and maneuvered our bodies into the perfect position for simultaneous blow jobs.

I moaned and nuzzled my nose against Xan's cock, buried it in his short, dark pubes, and breathed deeply.

Xan's tongue licked the sensitive spot at the crease of my groin before taking my cock in his hand and stroking slowly. "Gonna suck this beautiful cock so hard. Can't wait to taste you, swallow you, feel you explode in my mouth."

I took Xan's hard length in my fist and pressed my lips to his head before dipping my tongue into his slit. The salty bitterness filled my mouth as Xan's hiss filled the air. I slid my lips around Xan's cock just as his hot mouth took me deep.

The only thing better than the velvety smooth shaft sliding between my lips and filling my mouth was the amazing wet heat of Xan's mouth engulfing my dick.

Kissing Xan would always be top of my list, but sucking his gorgeous cock was definitely going to give kissing a run for its money. I wanted his cock in my mouth at all times. If he was okay with sucking me 24/7, I'd be in heaven.

Xan moved one hand to cup my balls while the other hand moved to grip my ass. I copied the move and soon we were gripping and fondling, sucking and thrusting, in a desperate rhythm. When Xan's finger teased into my ass and pressed against my hole, my balls drew up tight and I knew I wouldn't last much longer. I trailed my finger against his taint and rubbed. Xan moaned and fucked hard into my mouth. Within seconds, we were both coming hard.

I sucked and swallowed, savoring every drop Xan gave me.

Xan popped from my cock and licked me clean before moving to the head of the bed to lay his head on the pillow next to me.

"Holy fuck." Xan sighed. "That was fucking amazing. I'll suck your cock any and every time you offer. Is it weird that I want your dick in my mouth as often as possible?"

I laughed. "I may have had the same thought. I'll gladly blow you all day, every day."

"Better than kissing?" Xan leaned in and kissed me.

"Different than kissing," I murmured against his mouth, "I love them both. But how have I gone my whole life without a dick in my mouth?"

Xan snorted. "I was thinking the same. But, if I'm being honest, I'm really glad we're sharing these firsts."

My heart turned to mush. "Same," I whispered.

"Are we moving too fast?" Xan asked suddenly. "I mean, I'm completely on board with all the physical stuff, but I want to be sure I'm not pushing you too quickly."

I propped up on my elbow and ran my hand along Xan's cheek. "Not at all. We spent a lot of time getting to know each other, falling for each other, before we moved to the physical stuff. All of this seems natural and right. Probably because it's us; I'm not sure I would be as eager with someone else." I pulled him close and brushed a kiss over his lips. "But no, we're not moving too fast."

Xan smiled and kissed me back. "Then let's eat and shower. I've got plans for that pretty ass of yours later." He flicked his tongue against my lips as I laughed.

After carry-out from The Lizard—where Bode's and Sage's teasing grins nearly split their faces in two—we cuddled on the couch for a bit.

"You take the bathroom first. When you're done with whatever you need to do in private, holler and I'll jump in the shower with you." Xan had his arms around me, locked in front of my chest, as we lounged on the sofa.

For a moment, I wondered what he meant, then our conversation about rimming and ass play came to mind and it all made sense. Kinda awkward, but kinda awesome that we could easily talk about things like that. I turned and tipped my chin up for a kiss. "Don't fall asleep waiting for me."

"Never. Maybe I'll watch a video," Xan teased with a wink.

"As long as you know that's all a show for entertainment purposes and I'm a real person with real flaws and all that." Suddenly, all the unrealistic parts of porn videos had me feeling very self-conscious.

Xan cocked his head and frowned. "Hey, don't do that. There's no comparison. I'll take the real you over all of that any day."

I scoffed. "You'd rather have my pasty skin, unwaxed balls and ass, totally average cock, and potential to shoot my load within three seconds? Riiiight."

Xan laughed and kissed me. "Yes, you goof. If you *want* to wax your ass or balls, go for it, but I love your body just the way it is. Your cock is amazing. And I have a feeling we'll have to work on our stamina together because if you're blowing in three seconds, I'll likely go in two point five."

Maybe he was lying. Maybe they were just words.

Maybe I fell a little bit more in love with him at that moment.

I kissed him hard and headed toward the bathroom.

After smiling at what I assumed were recent additions to Xan's toiletries—it was sweet that he thought to get preparation supplies for us—I stripped down and took some time to prepare privately before turning on the shower. I cracked the door and yelled out, "I'm ready."

I laughed at how quickly a very naked Xan barged into the bathroom. "'Bout time, I was going crazy out there."

"Dude, I took like twenty minutes." I wrapped my arms around him and groaned when our cocks pressed together.

"That was twenty minutes I missed out on having you

in my arms." Xan kissed me and I shivered as the coarse hair on his chest teased against my nipples. "Cold? Get in the shower. I'll warm you up."

We spent the next several minutes in a steamy, sensual embrace. Arms and legs tangling, hands roaming, and tongues teasing.

"The problem with this shower is that it doesn't stay hot forever. We've got about five minutes before we lose the heat. Let's wash. Once we're out, I'll take a few moments and meet you in bed." Xan reached for the soap and worked it between his palms until he had a good froth. He handed me the bar, which I nearly dropped when his slick hands took my cock in his grasp and began to stroke.

"Fuck." I soaped my hands, returned the soap, and moved to wash Xan's heavy length.

"What? Washing is more fun if we share the job." Xan moved his hand to the cleft of my ass and pressed his soapy fingers between my cheeks. "Gonna eat this ass," he whispered hotly against my ear.

I whimpered and spread my legs to offer him better access.

Xan ran his fingers up and down my crease, from the top to my balls and back up. Then he pressed his slippery finger against my hole. "Gonna spread your legs and tease this pretty hole with my tongue."

"Damn, Xan." I fought the urge to position myself so he could rim me right there in the small shower stall. Xan was a dirty talker and it turned out I absolutely loved it.

I grabbed the soap and lathered my hands again before moving to Xan's ass. When I spread his cheeks and soaped his crease, Xan shuddered. He groaned when my fingers soaped his taint and moved slowly back to his hole.

"Want you to tongue fuck me." Xan rocked his hips. "Want you to fuck my face until you blow, then tongue my ass and suck me off while you play with my hole."

My knees nearly buckled. "Fuck, Xan. Your words are about to kill me."

"Don't die," Xan demanded. "We've got things to do. Important things, sexy things," he whispered against my mouth, "things I'm glad to be doing with only you. Makes it even better somehow."

Xan turned off the rapidly cooling water and we climbed from the shower.

I dried my hair and body quickly, smacked a kiss on Xan's lips, and reached for the door. "Don't leave me waiting too long." I gripped my hard length. "I may have to start on this without you."

Xan's dark eyes narrowed and he licked his lips. "Don't you dare."

I waggled my brows and left him alone in the bathroom. I grabbed a bottle of water and downed half of it before climbing into Xan's bed to wait. My cock was hard and heavy against my stomach, begging me to stroke it, but I waited for Xan. I passed the time by imagining the things Xan and I had talked about wanting to try. The images in my head did nothing to relieve my throbbing cock, but were entertaining nonetheless.

My eyes flew open when I heard the bathroom door open a while later. Xan's gorgeous skin was flushed, his thick cock bobbed against his stomach from a thatch of dark hair, and his smoldering eyes never left mine as he walked toward me. He crawled onto the bed and covered me with his body before capturing my mouth in a hot, wet kiss.

Our mouths mated for several moments before Xan pulled back. "I want your ass, roll over. Up on your knees." He waited for me to comply. "Spread your legs, let me see that pretty pucker."

I obeyed, shivering as the cool air kissed my exposed hole.

Xan knelt behind me, spread my ass, and pressed soft kisses from the top of my ass, over my opening, all the way down to the soft skin behind my balls. He returned quickly to my sensitive hole and flicked his tongue against my skin. With a moan, Xan flattened his tongue and pressed hard against me before rubbing, lapping, and finally pushing his tongue into me.

My arms and legs were not prepared to withstand the type of sensual torture Xan was doling out, and I collapsed onto the bed with a whimper.

Xan chuckled. He shifted to attack my ass with his tongue again and again until I was a shuddering, panting ball of nerves under him.

"Stop, Xan. Gotta stop, or I'll be done before we get to do anything else," I gasped.

Xan rolled from the bed and coaxed me into a standing position facing him. He kissed me with wet, swollen lips before dropping to his knees. "I want you to fuck my face. Hard. Use my mouth like a fuck hole and make me gag on your cock." His big, dark eyes looked up, pleading as if he was as shocked by the request as I was.

I nodded and Xan nuzzled my cock as he took hold of my hips.

"Hold my hair, pull it, give me all you've got," Xan said before he took my hard length in his hot mouth.

I began rocking my hips, thrusting slowly into his mouth, my balls already drawing up tight. But Xan shook his head and forced my hips into a faster, harder rhythm.

With Xan's fists guiding my hips, my cock hammering the back of his throat, and the wet sound of my dick slipping between his lips over and over, I knew I'd come in less than a minute. "Xan, I'm going to come. Stop if you don't want me to come."

Xan pulled off for just a moment, tears leaking from his eyes from the abuse his throat was taking, "Shoot your cum down my throat, I want it all." He took my dick back into his mouth and forced my hips into an even faster and harder rhythm until I couldn't hold off any longer.

With a groan, I exploded down Xan's throat. I shuddered at the extreme satisfaction it gave me to watch him gag on my cock and swallow as much of my cum as he could. I thumbed a bit that leaked from his lips and rubbed it against my lips.

Xan licked me clean and stood with a growl before attacking my mouth and licking the cum from my lips. "My turn," he murmured and pushed me to the bed. He straddled my chest and tapped his cock against my lips.

I teased the tip of his dick and moaned when I tasted his pre-cum. Opening my mouth, I reveled in the way Xan fed his cock between my lips and began to thrust slowly. I let him rock in and out several times before I sat up, knocking him off balance and onto his back.

I lifted his legs up and spread his knees to expose his hole. Gathering spit on my tongue, I pressed against his hole and swirled my tongue while Xan writhed and groaned. I licked from his hole to his taint, tongued his balls, and returned to tease his hole. When Xan gasped that it was too soon, I moved to his side and took his cock in my fist. I stroked him several times before slicking my finger with spit. As I moved my hand to his ass and pressed my wet digit against his tight pucker, I took his dick in my mouth and swallowed him as deeply as my gag reflex would allow. I slicked my finger again and pushed more spit into his ass as I bobbed on his cock.

Xan's body resisted as I pressed slowly against his tight ring. But soon, the muscle gave way and allowed my wet finger to slide inside. I sucked his cock and fingered his ass, loving the shudders that traveled through him and the moans escaping him.

"Fuck, Chase, gonna come," Xan growled.

Pulling from his cock, I repeated his words, "Shoot your cum down my throat, I want it all."

He roared and thrust his cock hard into my greedy mouth as his ass clenched around my finger. I swallowed his thick, hot cum, catching a bit that dribbled from my mouth with my finger and pressing Xan's cum into his pulsing hole. He whimpered and reached to pull me to his chest.

We lay together, panting for several moments.

"I gotta say some things if you're okay with that," Xan stated, still slightly breathless.

"Go for it. Unless you want to do that again too soon. I'm not on board. I don't think I can even walk right now."

Xan snorted. "Same. You may have killed me." He kissed the top of my head. "One, sex has *never* been this amazing. So whatever magic you're working on me, keep it up."

I chuckled. "It's my magic wand." I gripped my spent cock and wiggled it. It flopped pathetically and we both cracked up. "What's two?"

Xan took a deep breath. "This isn't just sex talking, promise. Although, as we've established, the sex is out of this world."

I waited.

"I don't care if this is too soon. I don't care if you can't join me. But I need to say this." Xan pressed a hand against my cheek and looked deep into my eyes. "Chase Steele, I'm not only falling in love with you. I'm already there. Full-fledged in love with you." He kissed me softly. "I love you. It's like you're what's been missing in my life this entire time. With you by my side, in my arms, everything makes more sense. It's okay if you don't feel the same yet," he started.

I gripped his chin and kissed him, horrified by the tears stinging in my eyes. "Stop, you big goof. Of course, I love you. It seems completely crazy to say this, but I one hundred percent understand what you mean. I knew my life was kinda fucked up and I missed out on a lot. What I didn't know was that one of the things missing was *you*. I needed you in my life like I needed my next breath. You're my best friend, my missing piece, my..." I paused.

"Boyfriend?" Xan offered.

I grinned and nodded before kissing him again. "Boyfriend. Perfect." I cuddled into Xan's arms and sighed. "That was amazing. All of it. The actions, the words, everything. I love you."

"I love you." Xan kissed the top of my head. "And we can do that again, right?"

"Fuck yeah," I said. "I mean, once I get feeling back to my extremities."

Xan laughed. "Same."

We drifted off to sleep.

# 16

## XAN

CHASE and I leaned against the bar, my arm subtly around his back, fingers grazing his side. It wasn't a full-on public display of affection, but I couldn't help wanting even just the slightest contact with him. The way he leaned into my body told me he wasn't against the touch.

The Salty Lizard was packed with happy party-goers ranging from infant to possibly even older than Bay's grandmother. Millie was approaching ninety if I wasn't mistaken, but a couple of attendees appeared to be pushing one hundred easily. Millie definitely didn't act like she was nearly a century old, so maybe she just seemed younger than some of the others.

Bode and Sage had closed The Lizard to the public for the private party. Millie refused to let them make the food and insisted on catering the party so Bode and Sage could enjoy themselves. Dinner had been delicious and Millie stood at the head table and clanged a spoon against the microphone. The racket got everyone's attention and she smiled.

"Bonnie and Ginny, come join me," Millie spoke into the microphone as she waved at her daughter and Chase's aunt. When the two women stood next to Millie, she continued. "We'd like to thank you for coming to our party. Life is short; relationships are important, and we wanted to celebrate life, friendships, and love." Millie gestured around the crowded room. "Look at all of you. You're so gorgeous, so special. These amazing, beautiful babies and children are our future. These men," she swept her hand toward the Silver crew, Chase, and me, "they are building lives, setting the corner stone of the future, and creating relationships to support each other, their children, the community." Millie paused and put her frail arm around Bonnie and Ginny. "Some of us are nearing the end of our watch, or at least reaching a point where we're more interested in handing over the reins to the younger generation. We wanted this party to reflect love, friendships, family—birth and chosen—trust, respect, memories of the past, and excitement for the future." Millie whispered something to Bonnie and Ginny who both shook their head. "Well, my cohorts don't want to talk, so you're stuck with me. We're going to have drinks, desserts, and dancing. If you're lucky, maybe I'll play storyteller. I have nearly a century of stories to tell," she paused and beamed toward Bay, "and some of them are *quite* entertaining."

Bay groaned.

Kyson tried to hide a smile.

Sage grinned.

Bode snorted.

"Before we get to the fun, I need to introduce some very important people." Millie moved to the middle of the bar, perched herself on a barstool, and crossed one leg over the other. "If I don't introduce a person here publicly, please make it your personal mission to meet them later as the party continues." She pointed a finger toward the whole room. "I mean it. I expect every single adult in this room to meet at least five new people. You never know if an introduction may lead to a new connection, new friendship, new love."

Millie spent the next several minutes introducing Bonnie and Ginny to the crowd. Then Bode and Sage, along with Oliver and Rosie. Next was Kyson, Bay, Arlo, and Cori. Benji and Rhys got an intro along with high praise for their art studio. I was touched when Millie introduced Chase and me to the whole crowd.

"These two are the perfect example of unexpected relationships. They ended up in the same area, surrounded by the same friends, and found themselves forming a strong friendship. I doubt either of them moved to Indianapolis looking for a friend, but look what fate handed them." Millie leaned forward and pretended to whisper, "And if you're as perceptive as this old gal, you've probably noticed how handsy and googly-eyed they've been with each other. A friendship forged in this beautiful city of ours has morphed into a gorgeous love." Millie tossed a smile to Chase and me. "Congratulations, you two. Nothing as grand as an unexpected love born from friendship."

The crowd clapped and the Silver crew hooted.

I tightened my arm around Chase's shoulder. "Well, that was slightly embarrassing," I whispered in his ear as I leaned closer.

"Only slightly?" Chase turned wide eyes my way. His face was a delicious shade of pink.

"At least it's over now. No awkwardness in telling the guys or answering nosey questions from guests." I kissed his cheek. "Millie did us a favor."

Chase chuckled. "The guys already knew. Hell, they knew before we did."

I shrugged. He wasn't wrong.

Millie finished her public introductions and turned off the microphone. People began to mill around as the promised drinks, desserts, and dancing began.

"This is a really great party. Kinda like a birthday party, frat party, wedding reception, and celebration of life all rolled into one." Chase glanced toward his aunt, Ginny. "I know this is pretty much her final farewell."

I took his hand and squeezed.

"I love that she's lived such a full life. Love that Rosie got to know her. Love that I got her back in my life." Chase pressed himself closer to me. "I just wish we all had more time."

I wrapped him in a hug. "I know." I kissed the top of his head. "She's an amazing person and she has two amazing kids. I'm so grateful to know her; grateful that she helped shape the man you are today. I hate that you don't have a lot of time left with her, but I love that you've got time to build some amazing memories for yourself and Rosie."

Chase shuddered in my arms and nodded against my shoulder.

"This is a party, no time for being sad." Ginny bumped into us with a hip. "Come on, the desserts are fabulous. And I better see you two dancing later. Part of this party was planned to nudge you boys together. Since you smartened up and took that step on your own, now it's the perfect time to enjoy yourselves." Ginny waggled her brows. "You know what Millie says about dancing." She laughed and moved on to chat with others.

Chase smiled.

"What does Millie say about dancing?" I asked.

He turned to me with eyes filled to the brim with a beautiful combination of love and lust. "That dancing is the perfect foreplay."

"Oh, really?" I raised my brow and gave him a smile. "I like the way she thinks."

Chase cupped his hand around my ear and leaned in close. "I want a few drinks, a couple desserts, and lots of dancing. Then later, I want to you to take advantage of this damn plug I've had in my ass this entire time and fuck me until I forget what day it is."

I nearly gave myself whiplash turning to look at Chase. "You're kidding, right?"

Chase grinned and bit his lip before attempting to school his features into a serious look. "I don't joke about desserts. Did you *see* that cinnamon roll?"

"Chase," I growled. "Are you wearing a butt plug right now?" I asked in a hissed whisper.

He pursed his lips and tapped a finger against his chin. "I guess you'll have to find out later. Let's go mingle. I want *allll* the drinks and desserts." He took my hand and pulled me into the crowd as he spoke of splitting a cinnamon roll and white cake with white icing.

I could barely fucking breathe as I thought about what this evening was possibly leading to. But Chase wanted to eat, drink, and dance first. I took a deep breath, willed my cock to behave, and followed him to the open bar.

* * *

Rhys approached the area where Bode, Sage, Kyson, Bay, Chase, and I were chatting over drinks. Next to him was one of the most strikingly beautiful men I'd ever seen. Tall, lean, perfectly coiffed hair, flawless brows that arched just right over cobalt blue eyes, and plump pink lips.

"I'd be jealous of you drooling, but I'm doing the same. Who is that?" Chase whispered.

I shook my head. "No clue. Not to worry, he's pretty, but I've got eyes for only you."

"Awww, so sweet." Chase kissed my cheek.

Rhys and the mystery man stopped in front of us. "Gentlemen, glad I caught all of you together."

It was weird how much my heart warmed every time the Silver guys included Chase and me in their crew. They just automatically accepted both of us and fit us right into their lives like we'd always been there. Their acceptance, trust, and friendship were as important to me as Chase's love; all things I'd never known I was missing until I had a taste of them and realized I couldn't live without them.

"I wanted to introduce you to my nephew, Tyler Golden. My sister, Caroline, is his mother." Rhys waited a moment while Tyler shook hands with the whole crew.

"I mostly go by Ty. And my full last name is Golden-Mann." He wrinkled his nose. "But I dropped the hyphen and Mann when I was eighteen. One, it's a mouthful. Two, I *may* be a golden boy," he winked, "but no need to advertise it."

We all laughed.

"What do you do?" Bode asked.

"Mostly a student." Ty answered smoothly, but I didn't miss the quick glance he gave his uncle.

"What are you studying?" Sage asked.

"I'm in cosmetology school."

"Like hair, makeup, nails?" Sage asked.

"Yeah, mostly hair and makeup." Ty nodded.

"Are you around here? I'm always down for a hair, makeup, and nails day." Sage sighed. "Sounds like heaven."

"You never said you wanted that." Bode frowned and elbowed Sage. "I'll take you."

"You want to get your hair, makeup, and nails done?" Sage raised a brow.

Bode shrugged. "No, but I'd take you."

"No need. My new friend Ty can take care of me. He's a professional."

Bode narrowed his eyes, glanced between Sage and Ty, then rolled his eyes with a sigh. "Fine. Have fun. The kids and I will hit the park or go watch a movie."

My insides fluttered a bit. *That* was the type of relationship I wanted. With Chase. I took his hand and gave it a squeeze. The way he squeezed mine in return made me think he was having the same thoughts.

"Dude, you would have ripped my head off a few years ago if Sage had indicated he wanted to spend a day with me," Bay groused. "What gives?"

Bode started to argue, cocked his head to the side, and frowned. "I guess I've grown up and know that I don't need to worry about losing Sage." He shrugged. "Plus, Ty may not even be gay. And he's not really Sage's type."

"Sage is *right here*," Sage said with a huff. *"We're married and I trust Sage ten thousand percent* was the only answer needed in this situation."

"Um, Ty is most definitely gay," Ty piped up. "And fabulous." He popped a hip dramatically and tossed a pretend mane. "To answer the original question, I'm right here in Indy."

"Awesome, I will definitely get your information and set up some appointments. How close are you to graduating?" Sage asked.

"Within four to six months. I've got a few salons interested in me because they've seen my work through some internships I've had around town, so I'm really anxious to finish and get a career started."

"You live nearby?" Bay asked.

Ty glanced toward Rhys.

"Actually, yes, very nearby," Rhys said. "He's taking the apartment above the studio."

"It's not a huge, fancy apartment, but it's definitely livable. Ty's going to help with some of the odd hours at the studio when Benji and I need to be creating instead of running the floor. Aside from his skills with hair and makeup, he's also got some fun art pieces he'll display on the floor."

"Perfect plan." Kyson nodded.

Before the group could fall into a comfortable chat, Benji and another man joined us.

"Ah, perfect timing," Rhys said and kissed Benji.

"So, I see you've already met Ty." Benji kissed Ty's cheek. "I wanted to introduce Victor Black to the whole clan."

The man, Victor, was very handsome. He struck me as

refined, possibly from money. At least that was the vibe I got. Victor was definitely older than most of us, although I'd wager Bay was slightly older by maybe five or six years. Vic wasn't broad, but he looked like he took care of himself. His salt-and-pepper hair was longer on top and swept back and to the side. He had a bit of scruff, thin lips that revealed straight, white teeth when he smiled, and golden-brown eyes.

"Call me Vic." He took time to shake everyone's hand. "It's nice to meet you all."

"Vic is a friend of my sister's. He's going to take some hours at the studio to help us out. Plus, he does amazing crochet and knit work and is available for commissioned work." Rhys placed a hand on Vic's shoulder.

"Vic, this is Ty, he's the one who will be living upstairs." Benji pulled Ty closer. "Gotta say, I love that you'll be living there, but I'm gonna miss being able to crash up there."

Rhys snorted. "Crashing there? Is that all you'll miss that apartment for?"

Ty wrinkled his nose. "I need to never hear another word of your fuck pad again. It's now my humble abode and I do *not* want to hear of any of my uncle's sexcapades happening there."

The whole group finally broke apart and mingled while enjoying drinks and desserts.

By the time the deejay dimmed the lights and turned up the music, I was just slightly buzzed and on a very happy sugar-high. Perfect combo to actually get me on the dance floor.

"So, I should probably tell you I'm not much of a

dancer," I murmured in Chase's ear as we neared the dancers bopping around the floor to the chicken dance.

Chase laughed. "Neither am I. I was picturing more slow song dancing."

"Everyone loves a good line dance," the deejay announced. "My friend, Ty, is going to help me out with The Cupid Shuffle. Just listen to the words if you don't already know it. Watch Ty if you're unsure what to do."

Ty took his place in front of the group as several eager participants joined him. The music began and I glanced toward Chase.

He shrugged with a smile.

We joined the group and followed the directions.

By the end of the song, Chase and I were both laughing at how *not* talented we were at dancing.

The deejay took a brief break to chat with Bode for a moment and we meandered off the floor. Soon, a slow song flowed from the speakers. The children didn't seem to notice the change in rhythm and continued to bounce around happily. But several couples moved to the floor and began to sway to the music.

I held my hand out to Chase and nodded my head toward the dance floor in question.

The way his face broke into a smile as he took my hand was something I wanted to experience every day for the rest of my life.

We took our place on the outskirts of the crowd—I had plans on whispering naughty things in his ear and didn't need others overhearing—and Chase wrapped his arms around my midsection. I settled my arms around his waist. We moved slowly to the music for several moments until Chase moved his arms to my shoulders. He rested his head on his elbow and kissed my jaw.

"This is the first time I've ever slow danced with anyone." Chase's admission surprised me.

"No high school dances?" I whispered gruffly.

"Not that I attended. Didn't have money for a ticket or clothes or flowers for a date. By high school, I was so focused on the Army, I did little outside of that. Spent most of my time making my escape plans." Chase shrugged. "What about you? King of the high school dance?"

"Oh, hell no." I nuzzled my chin against the top of his head. "I was never placed in a foster home long enough to build friendships or be wanted at a dance. And the clubs I moved between definitely weren't putting on dances." I pulled him close. "I danced with a couple girls who took me to weddings as their date—mostly as shock value—but you're the first guy I've ever danced with." I kissed his ear. "And first person I've ever *wanted* to hold in my arms while a random song plays."

"You and your sweet words," Chase teased.

"Oh, I've got some words for you." I ran a hand up and down his back.

Chase moved so his mouth was right by my ear. "I love your dirty talk so feel free to share your words with me as much as you want." He pressed his cheek against mine.

"You're a fucking tease and horrible person to tell me you're wearing a plug," I growled against his ear.

"Now, now," Chase murmured, "I thought it could be a nice little addition to the dancing foreplay. It definitely caught your attention."

"We're going to dance for a few more songs, then I'm dragging you back to my place," I promised.

"We could just go upstairs," Chase suggested.

"No way. The things I plan on us doing have no place around children. Even behind closed doors."

Chase made a needy little noise in my ear. "That sounds promising."

"I'm going to strip you naked and play with the plug in your pretty ass. I want to watch it slide in and out as your hole stretches. Gonna imagine your body opening for my cock." I pressed a kiss against his ear as a second slow song came on. "Then I'll slick up my cock, pull the plug out, and push my cock into your ass. Watch your body stretch around me, open for me, feel your tight heat."

Chase whimpered and tightened his arms around me as our hardening cocks brushed together as we continued to dance.

"You think you'll want me to fuck you soft and slow or hard and fast?"

"I want to try both, but I have a feeling that I'll want hard and fast tonight. Fuck, Xan, I could come in my pants right now."

"My cock will fill you so full, throbbing inside you until I blow and fill you with my cum," I whispered. "Then I'll pull out slowly, suck your pretty cock, and roll to straddle you." My imagination played out the scene. "I want to sit on your dick, feel you stretch me, ride your cock as you thrust hard and deep in my ass."

"We need to leave." Chase demanded. "Now. Come on. We say our goodbyes and get the fuck to your place." He took my hand and led me to Bode and Sage.

Despite the knowing smirks from almost every person

we made our excuses to, Chase never once faltered. The process of saying goodbye helped to calm my raging libido a bit. By the time we left The Lizard, I was still horny as hell, but I appreciated the moment to gather my wits.

"I know we talked about our recent blood work being clear. Do we want to discuss the use of condoms?" Chase broached the subject as we walked down the block.

"If you were someone I'd just met, or if one—or both —of us had a reason to insist on condoms, or if we weren't planning to be monogamous, I'd say condoms for sure." I spoke my thoughts. "But we both got clear tests. Neither of us have been with anyone else in several months."

Chase snorted. "*Several* is very accurate."

"And we're monogamous, right? Just us? No others?"

Chase took my hand as we approached the apartment. "Definitely. I'm fine with or without condoms, just thought it was best to discuss it before we made our way to hot and heavy in bed."

"I say we go without if we're in agreement."

"Agreed." Chase took the key from my shaky hand and unlocked the door. "Now, I believe you have some words to re-enact." He pulled his shirt over his head.

We each lost articles of clothing as we kissed and walked toward the bed.

"Get on the bed and spread your legs, I want to see," I demanded.

Chase crawled onto the mattress, rolled to his back, planted his feet, and spread his legs.

The black silicone plug beckoned me like a moth to a flame. My breath caught in my chest and I ran a finger over the visible part of the toy. I reached for the lube and tossed it on the bed. "This is sexy as fuck. How does it feel?"

"It stung a bit at first. But I was so turned on thinking about taking your cock that it quickly became a good pain. Hardly even notice it now." Chase stroked his cock.

I took hold of the silicone and slid it slowly from his body.

"Okay, definitely notice it now." Chase gasped. "Fuuuck that's good."

"Love your ass, so perfect." I couldn't tear my eyes from Chase's hole; the way it stretched and took the plug. "Gonna be my dick sliding in here soon."

Chase whimpered. "God, yes. Want that, want to feel you stretch my hole and fill me."

As I worked the toy in and out, I fondled Chase's balls. "Want to come in you, want to see my cum dripping from your ass."

He shuddered. "Please, Xan. Need more, want to feel you."

I moved to fit myself between Chase's spread legs and rubbed our cocks together as I leaned close to capture his mouth in a kiss. "How do you want it?"

"I think like this." Chase tongued my bottom lip. "Want to see your face when you're fucking me."

"I love you," I whispered against this mouth.

"Love you." Chase rocked his hips. "Now fuck me."

I sat back on my knees and grabbed the lube to drizzle on my cock. The position likely wasn't the easiest for our first time, but the image of Chase's legs wrapped around me as I fucked into him was enough to have me leaking pre-cum over my fist as I stroked myself.

I slowly removed the plug from Chase's body and

watched in fascination as his hole quivered as if longing for the fullness the plug provided. I tossed the toy to the side and pressed my cock head against his pretty pucker. As I slid in, my slick cock filling his ass inch-by-inch, Chase threw his head back and moaned.

"So full, you're so thick," Chase panted out his words as he leaned up on his elbows to watch me take his ass.

"Is it too much?" I slowed.

"Don't you dare stop."

I pushed in deeper until my balls pressed against Chase's warm skin. "Fuck, you're so damn tight. So hot," I growled. "You good?"

"So damn good. Move, please. Want to feel you thrusting into me. Fuck me."

I shifted and Chase wrapped his legs around my back as I began a slow, hard rhythm thrusting into his body. "Fuck, so good."

Chase yelped when I pressed in deeper.

"You okay?"

"Yeah, do that again." Chase's words were slurred.

I slid in deep and held my hips in place as Chase whimpered. "Hit the right spot, huh?" I teased.

"Mmhm, so right. Fuck, that's so good."

I continued to fuck into him, increasing the pace as I wrapped my arms under his shoulders and held tight. "Gonna come, can't wait. Jerk yourself."

Chase took his cock in his hand. "Do it, come in me," he demanded as he stroked himself.

"Wanna see you come first," I gritted out.

I watched as Chase stroked his throbbing cock until he threw his head back and painted his belly and chest.

The sight of Chase coming, and the way his ass

clenched around my cock, brought me to a roaring release and I pumped into his ass hard. I pulled from him slowly and groaned as my cum leaked from his hole. I used my dick to push it back in and fuck him slowly until I collapsed on him in a sweaty, cum-covered mess.

"Want to do that over and over," Chase murmured. "Not right this second, but soon."

"You're so fucking sexy, watching you take me like that was amazing." I pulled from his body and gathered him close. "Would love to switch; want to feel your cock in my ass, too. If you're down."

"As much as you seemed to enjoy it, I'm definitely down." Chase kissed me. "That was *really* good, thank you. I'd never realized sex could be that...intense."

"For me, too. I think maybe we were both just missing something and now we have it." I tipped his chin and kissed him deep and slow. "Let's shower and sleep. Need to build up energy for the next round."

After a shower, Chase and I took turns rimming and sucking each other off before we fell to sleep wrapped in a cocoon of arms and blankets.

\* \* \*

One thing I'd learned fairly quickly about Chase as he'd started to sleep over from time to time was that he slept like the dead.

When I woke the next morning, I savored the warmth of our naked bodies wrapped together. My morning wood was already making itself known and Chase's erection pressed against my thigh. With a wicked grin, I decided to wake him up properly.

I shimmied under the blanket, running my nose along the skin of his abdomen, until I reached his cock. Breathing him in deep, I cupped his balls and took his length between my lips. Chase stirred slightly as I began to suck, but didn't wake. As I continued to take his cock deep, I teased his taint and balls.

I knew the exact moment Chase came fully awake by the way his body tensed and the low "Fuuuuck" he breathed out slowly.

I popped off his cock and smiled up at him from under the blanket he'd just lifted. "Good morning."

"You're wicked." Chase touched my face. "I love it."

After licking the broad head of his cock once more, I moved up to face him. "I'm thinking I want to try bottoming. May like it, may not, but I'll never know unless I try. You game?"

Chase's nostrils flared and he nodded. "Get the lube."

I reached for the bottle we'd discarded on the bedside table last night before straddling Chase's hips. "I think this position may be best for me since I didn't get to spend all day with a plug in my ass."

"Your fault, not mine." Chase winked and smiled. "I can hook you up with my supplier."

I narrowed my eyes. "If it's Millie or Bode, I'm gonna pass. Can't see that conversation actually taking place."

Chase laughed. "It's not. I found it online. Arrives in discreet packaging and everything."

"Well, that's a relief. The last thing I need is for the mail carrier or anyone at the shop seeing a box addressed to me with BUTT PLUG stamped all over it." I flipped the cap and drizzled lube on my fingers before reaching behind me to coat my hole.

Chase held out his hand and I poured a bit into his palm so he could slick his cock. "It's okay if we don't do this, I'm not going to be upset if I *have* to bottom all the time. I'll take one for the team; I'm a good person like that."

I smirked. "You're so generous and self-sacrificing. Makes me want to do it more; has to be amazing."

Using his slick fingers, Chase breached me with first one and then a second digit. The burning stretch took my breath away, but I immediately wanted more.

"Do a third," I bit out.

He groaned and added a third finger to my ass.

I gasped and enjoyed the way he worked me open for a moment before I couldn't take it any longer. I reached for Chase's cock and positioned it at my entrance. "Need you in me."

"Just go slow," Chase advised.

I pressed down and the broad head of his cock pushed against me. For a moment, I freaked out. Maybe I should just slick up and slide into Chase. We knew we both liked that. No. I needed to know. I lowered myself a bit more and groaned. The stretch of my hole around Chase's cock was so much more than when I'd opened for his fingers.

Chase rubbed one palm along my thigh and stroked my rapidly flagging dick with his other. "You're doing so good. Taking me so good," Chase murmured, but I saw the concern on his face.

With one last press against his cock—and I was forever grateful that Chase controlled himself and didn't thrust into me like I'm sure he wanted to—my body's resistance gave way and accepted him completely.

"Fuuuck," I breathed out. "So damn huge. So full."

"Oh God, you're so hot and tight," Chase panted as he gripped my hips.

"Go slow, but move, please." I leaned forward, hands on either side of Chase's shoulders.

Chase began to thrust up his hips, pumping into me, stretching me, and—holy mother of God—hitting something inside just right until I saw stars. As I shuddered and nearly collapsed, Chase laughed.

"Yeah, that spot's pretty great, huh? Had me almost drooling last night." He pumped deep again. "You good?"

I nodded. "Go faster."

"Sit back a bit, wanna watch you ride me."

I obeyed. I settled into a medium rhythm as Chase placed one hand on my hip and one on my cock. He stroked in perfect timing with each deep thrust of his cock into my heat.

"Wanna come in your ass. You gonna come this way?" Chase thumbed my slit.

"Come in me. Then I want to jack off all over you." I gripped my hand over Chase's and stroked.

He gripped my hips with both hands and began thrusting hard and fast and deep. Over and over, until he roared his release and his throbbing cock unloaded in my ass.

I pumped my cock hard, imagining what my hole looked like, stretched wide for Chase's cock, dripping with his cum. That was all it took. I groaned as my cock exploded white ropes of cum all over his chest and chin. Leaning forward, I licked his chin and then kissed him, slow and deep.

"Good morning," I murmured.

"I think I could get used to waking up like this every

day." Chase wrapped his arms around me as his softening cock slipped from my body. "Was that okay? Did you like it?"

"It was great. I wasn't sure what to expect, but I did like it." I kissed him again. "But I'm down for you doing it more than me since you seemed to like it even more."

Chase's cheeks pinked. "Who knew I'd be a greedy little bottom?"

"Fuck, why does that totally turn me on?" I shifted to my side and wrapped my arms around Chase. "It's early. Let's sleep a bit." I kissed the top of his head. "Thank you for that. I love you."

"Love you, too," Chase murmured against my chest sounding as if he was already drifting off to sleep.

## 17

## CHASE

"MMM, I love a man who can cook," Xan whispered as he nibbled my ear while looking over my shoulder.

"I turned on the crock-pot this morning. I don't know that I'd count that as cooking. Sage had it all prepared." I checked the time on the pot. "If the rolls turn out well, I'll take credit for those. It's only letting them rise and then popping them in the oven, but I have high hopes."

"Well, it smells delicious. Thank you for inviting me over." Xan kissed my cheek.

"Are you guys *boyfriends?*" Rosie piped up from her perch at the kitchen bar where she was coloring next to Oliver.

"Yes," I hedged and my heart soared when Xan took my hand.

"I'm going to have a boyfriend." Rosie returned to her coloring.

"I'm not having a boyfriend *or* a girlfriend," Oliver stated. "Yuck. Kissing is gross."

"I hear that we'll probably change our minds about

that when we're grownups." Rosie shrugged. After finishing the unicorn she was coloring like a rainbow, she replaced a purple crayon to the box. "I don't want a boyfriend for kissing. I just need him to take me places and buy me stuff."

Xan laughed.

"She's not wrong," I teased.

He put me in a headlock. "I think you like me for more than just that if last night was any indication," he whispered softly.

"Behave," I admonished, "but you're also not wrong."

"Are we going to the park?" Oliver asked suddenly.

I checked the clock. "Yes, we can go for an hour, but then it's home for dinner."

The kids donned light hoodies and we headed down the stairs. With Oliver and Rosie skipping along ahead of us and Xan and I holding hands as we walked down Mass. Ave., I was once again struck with the thought of *How the hell is this my life*? I wasn't complaining. I wasn't wanting it to be anything different. I was just in awe—daily—that my circumstances had changed so much for the better in such a short time.

I gave Xan's hand a squeeze. I was definitely a blessed and lucky man. Who knew that coming to Indy would change my entire life?

As fall gave one last show of colors before turning brown and heading into winter, the days were beginning to get slightly shorter and somewhat cooler, but there were still a couple hours of sunshine left and the kids loved any chance to play at the park.

Xan and I waved to Oliver and Rosie when they turned to see if we were keeping up.

"I kinda love their energy," Xan remarked. "And it kinda wears me out."

I chuckled. "Yeah, I don't remember ever having that much energy or being so carefree."

"You and I grew up different; we probably never were that carefree." Xan squeezed my hand. "But I love that they both have better than we had."

My heart warmed. "Yeah, that's a great way to look at it. I've spent so much time regretting a past I couldn't control. It's time to move on from that. My past made me who I am, and I truly believe that everything in my past led me here to find Ginny and Rosie, the Silvers, and you. How could I regret that?"

The kids waited at the crosswalk while we caught up. Once we crossed the road, they took off running into the park.

"Playground first, stay where we can see you," I hollered.

"I like that." Xan nodded as we followed the kids. "I was so angry at my mom, my dad, every foster family who gave up on me. But all of that made me who I am and eventually brought me here. Great city, great job, great friends, great boyfriend." He bumped his hip against mine. "I think I'm tired of being angry at the past; I'm ready to be content with the present and excited for the future."

"Love that." I kissed his cheek. "Love you."

We spent the next twenty minutes watching the kids run between the swings, the jungle gym, and the slides.

"Can we go to the obstacle course?" Oliver asked breathlessly as he ran to our bench with Rosie hot on his heels.

"Sure thing. You've got about fifteen minutes there. Then we can feed the ducks before we head back home." It was so surreal to be acting as a parent figure and having an actual *home* to return to. I wasn't ready for kids of my own, but helping to take care of my sister and Oliver was definitely something I found myself falling in love with.

The kids raced to what they'd deemed the obstacle course. It did have a lot of paths, slides, nets, ladders, poles, stairs, bridges, and the like, so I was sure it did seem like a challenge to little ones.

"I'll go grab duck food and meet you at the pond. Save a trip to the vendor and back." Xan gestured to the other side of the duck pond.

"Sounds good."

As our time drew to an end, I hollered at the kids that they could do one last run through the course. I glanced across the pond for Xan.

I frowned.

At first, I couldn't find him.

The park wasn't crowded. He should have been easy to find.

Then I caught sight of him near a grove of trees.

Talking to someone.

Xan held the duck food in his hands, but his posture was tense.

What the hell?

Who was he talking to?

I couldn't see the man's face, just his back.

The kids came running.

"Ducks!" Rosie shrieked with laughter.

She and Oliver took off toward the little dock on the other side of the pond.

I followed, keeping my eyes on the kids *and* Xan as I walked. I didn't like it. It wasn't jealousy coursing through me. Xan definitely wasn't flirting. He was angry. The situation felt weird and off.

By the time I caught up with the kids, Xan had stormed away from the man and plastered a smile on his face while holding out the duck food.

"Let's feed the quackers and then get home to feed you two quackers," Xan teased, although his smile didn't reach his eyes.

"Everything good?" I asked in a low voice while the kids stepped onto the dock to toss their pieces to the noisy water fowl.

"Yeah, not a problem anyone needs to worry about." Xan took and deep breath and kissed my cheek.

"That's the first time in our friendship that you've lied to me." I frowned. "I knew it would hurt, but it's worse than I thought."

Xan sighed. "It was a guy from my past. Old club leader. Just sayin' hi."

I stared deep in his eyes for a moment. "When you're ready to tell me the truth, I'm here. I'm guessing it's kinda scary; he looked pretty threatening. I don't like you lying to me, but I can give you some time to wrap your head around whatever he said to you. I want us to face that kind of shit together. Just don't take too long."

Xan closed his eyes and pulled me close. "I love you. I don't deserve you, but I'm so damn glad I have you. Let's go eat."

"We still working on the bike later?" I asked.

"Definitely. You staying over?"

"Still want me to?"

"Always." He kissed the top of my head.

I nodded into his chest.

The kids scrambled toward us. "We're done!"

"Then let's go eat!" I smiled. I knew Xan was lying, but I also knew in my heart that he was scared. I'd give him some time. I could do that. *What if he never tells you the truth? Is that any way to build a relationship?* I pushed the niggling thoughts to the back of my mind.

\* \* \*

"Dinner was delicious," Bode said as he swiped a napkin across his mouth. "Thank you so much for starting the food and keeping an eye on the kids. Sage and I had a ton of inventory and paperwork to catch up on downstairs. You were a huge help."

"And the rolls were absolutely perfect," Xan added.

Bode laughed. "As evident by the fact that both kids ate like four rolls. Sage is lucky he's getting the last two."

"I thought it was crazy to fix two packs, but the way the kids scarfed them down showed me the error of my thinking." I stood and pushed back my chair from the table.

"You two help with your part of clearing the table," Bode instructed the kids.

Oliver and Rosie picked up their silverware, placed the pieces gently on their plates, and walked them to the kitchen.

When the three men followed with our own plates, we found Oliver scraping the plates into the trash while Rosie stood on a stool and rinsed the plates and utensils with the sprayer.

I packed up a little to-go type container with food for Sage as Xan and Bode loaded the dishwasher. The kids collected napkins, condiments, and cups from the table.

Within twenty minutes, dinner was completely cleared and the kitchen was cleaned. I turned on the dishwasher and Xan gathered up the trash bag to run down to the dumpster.

"He seems weird." Bode watched Xan walk out the door. "You both kinda do."

I shrugged. "He saw someone from his past at the park today. Seems to have messed with his head. He's not telling me everything and it's bothering me."

Bode pursed his lips. "Give him some time, let him know you're there and support him. He's used to dealing with things on his own; probably doesn't know how to handle discussing his issues with someone else."

I gave some thought to his words. Bode wasn't wrong. In fact, I'd been so used to dealing with my own problems with no one to turn to—until the guys and Xan and Ginny —that I probably wouldn't have known what to do if I was in the same situation. "Yeah, you're right. It just worries me that he's so shaken up by it."

"You'll work it out. Keep the communication open. Best advice." Bode slapped me on the shoulder. "Also, sex is always a good way to relieve stress."

I laughed. "I'll keep that in mind." Sex with Xan was always on my mind. I'd decided—before the day's weirdness—that I was going to initiate a bit of something a little rougher than what we'd done before. I loved what we'd been doing, but I was feeling adventurous and completely trusted Xan to be rough with me without actually hurting me.

Xan returned. "It's thundering. I think we're going to get a storm. You want to head to the shop?"

"You good if I leave?" I asked Bode.

"Yep, the kids and I will take food to Sage. One of us will come back up and do bedtime with them." Bode picked up the container of food for Sage. "Thank you both again for your help. Really appreciate you and glad we have two people we can trust to love and care for our kids as much as we do."

I noticed a small crease on Xan's forehead as Bode spoke, but he smiled it away and just nodded. "Sure thing, always down for helping with these monkeys." Xan ruffled Rosie's and Oliver's hair.

Rosie shrieked and flung herself around Xan's waist for a hug.

Oliver wasn't a super demonstrative kid with anyone other than his dads, but he leaned into me and let me put an arm around his shoulder.

"'Night, kiddo. Have a good day at school tomorrow." I gave him a gentle squeeze.

Once Rosie had her fill of hugging Xan—believe me, girl, I know—she jumped into my arms, wrapping her legs around my waist and smacking a kiss on my cheek. "G'night, Chasey." She giggled at her own silliness.

I hugged her close and watched over her shoulder as Oliver approached Xan. My heart, already bursting with having my baby sister in my life, almost exploded when Xan knelt down and held his fist out to Oliver.

"Fist bump," Xan offered.

Oliver glanced toward Bode as if looking for reassurance.

Bode nodded.

Oliver grinned slightly and bumped his little fist against Xan's.

Once goodbyes were said, Xan and I hurried down the stairs and out into the early evening.

"I love thunderstorms, but I'd rather not be stuck walking in one," Xan exclaimed as a huge clap of thunder shook the air around us. "Make a run for it?" He held his hand out to me.

I took it and we began to run just as huge drops of rain started splatting against the sidewalk. Fall thunderstorms weren't *as* impressive as summer ones, but this one sounded like it was going to be a pretty big one—or at least a loud one.

We reached Whitfield's just as the sky ripped open and a deluge began.

Laughing, we ran inside and listened as the rain pounded the windows and tin roof. Xan grabbed two ciders from the fridge and flipped on the little radio we'd bought for our work bay.

"Guess no one else is working tonight," I observed.

Xan shrugged. "Or they went to dinner and will work later."

We set up the tools we'd need for the evening's work and Xan showed me a few images of what we would be doing with the chain and sprockets. Once he'd given a brief explanation, we got to work.

"Think we'll be finished in time for warm weather?" I asked.

"Definitely. She only needed the simplest of fixes. Another few weeks and we'll have her up and running like she was meant to. Then we'll have all winter to work on the detailing and custom work." Xan winked, bumped my shoulder, then handed me a wrench. "We'll be ready to ride by the first warm day. Gonna be great."

"I've loved working on the bike like this. I may have to get another one; it's kinda addicting."

Xan laughed. "Told ya. I'm definitely down for rebuilding another one. Maybe make a profit from it and keep putting most of the profit toward the next one."

"That sounds really good. Let's plan on it." I paused until Xan glanced my way. "You're planning on being around, right?"

He frowned. "Yeah, of course. Why?"

"Just wondered. I know seeing that guy kinda fucked with your head."

Xan ran a hand over his face. "Look, I'm not purposely trying to keep things from you. Chrome—that's the guy from the park—he came to ask me to do some work for the club. My first reaction was to tell him to fuck off, but he gave me a lot to think about. I need some more time to process it before I give him an answer."

We worked quietly for a few moments. "Way I see it, gut reactions usually keep us alive. Just be safe." I leaned over and kissed him softly. "Just remember you're not on your own anymore."

Xan relaxed into the kiss. When we broke apart, he rested his forehead against mine. "Thanks. It's a good reminder."

As Xan returned to working, I trailed a finger over one of his tattoos. "I love your ink so much."

"Could have your own," Xan suggested and watched me with a raised brow when I didn't immediately and vehemently refuse.

"Thing is, I love tattoos and would love some of my

own. The fear of needles is the only thing stopping me." I shuddered. "It's bad enough when I have to do medical procedures and tests. Why would I voluntarily put myself under a needle when I *know* the anxiety it brings?"

Xan smirked. "Maybe it would help you to see what a tattoo gun looks like, watch me get one, see that the needles aren't like shot needles, and they aren't going deep in your skin."

I started to protest, but I stopped when I realized that I actually had no idea what a tattoo gun looked like or even what getting a tattoo even consisted of. "That actually isn't a bad idea."

"You know, if you ever decide to get one, I'd go with you and keep you distracted. The pain isn't terrible; some people actually find it relaxing."

"So, it's not like having to get a million shots or IV's?"

Xan chuckled. "Nah. It's more like a fine point pen writing on a sunburn."

I imagined what he was describing. "Well, that doesn't sound pleasant, but it's a lot better than what my head had convinced me it's like."

"Just say the word; I'm here to help in whatever way." Xan pressed into my side.

"Are we almost to a stopping point?"

He glanced around at the parts and pieces. "Um, yeah, we can pause here. Why?"

I wrapped my arms around his neck and whispered in his ear. "Because I kinda want to go upstairs, shower, and have you fuck me so hard I'm walking a bit funny at work tomorrow."

Xan gripped my hips, pulled our bodies together, and kissed me. "I'm down."

"I mean it, I want it rough." My face flamed, but I knew I could trust Xan with my desires.

"Don't want to hurt you," Xan murmured against my lips as his rock-hard dick rubbed against me.

"You'd never hurt me. I trust you. Just need you like that." I pressed my forehead against his. "If you're okay with it."

"Help me clean up," Xan commanded.

We had the bay completely cleared within mere moments.

Within thirty minutes we'd prepped, showered, and fallen into bed in a hot, damp knot of arms and legs.

"Hard and fast?" Xan asked expectantly.

I nodded. "Harder than the usual hard. I don't want anything truly harmful, but I want to feel the pain. Know you're there to soothe the hurt."

"I want you to tell me if anything is too much." Xan cupped my face. "And I need you to know that I love you very much. If you're not too sore, I want to make love to you after this."

My heart soared. "I love you. I don't even completely understand my need for this, but I want it and I only want it with you." I kissed him. "You make love to me every time we're together, no matter how hard or soft it is."

"Can I tie up your arms?" Xan ran a hand over my chest.

With a thick swallow, I nodded.

Xan moved away and rifled through his closet. He emerged with a necktie and a sly smile. "Do I get to decide where we do this?"

Again, all I could do was nod.

"Move to the couch. Knees on the cushion, chest on

the arm, put your arms behind your back." Xan's gruff words were like gasoline on the fiery inferno already burning me from the inside.

I rolled from the bed and moved to the position he'd described on the couch.

"Tell me if this is too tight," Xan whispered in my ear as he began to secure my wrists together. "Gonna eat this pretty ass and bring you so close before I slam my cock deep in your hole, stretch you, fill you, and fuck you so hard."

Damn Xan and his dirty talk. My cock dripped precum and my pucker clenched in anticipation.

Xan kissed my neck and down my back. After biting each ass cheek, he spread me wide and tickled my hole with his hot breath. He teased around my hole until I was begging.

"Please, Xan, fuck me with your tongue," I begged.

Xan relented and dipped his warm tongue into my body. He teased and tasted, pressed and licked, sucked and kissed my most sensitive part until my knees barely held me up.

"Look at that pretty pucker, all soft and open for my cock, just waiting to be filled," Xan murmured as he pumped lube onto his hand. After he coated his cock and my hole, Xan pressed against me.

"Hard, Xan. Please, I need it." I pushed my hips back.

Xan entered me in one hard, fast thrust.

I gasped as the swift pain threatened to overtake me, but it soon eased. I shifted on the cushion and spread my knees farther apart.

Xan wrapped an arm around my chest and pulled me up until my back was flush against his front. "Your hole is so damned hot. Pulling me in deep, clinging to me, begging for more of this fat cock." He used both hands to pinch my nipples.

When I groaned, Xan pinched harder. The pain went straight to my dick.

He kept one hand on my nipple and moved the other to stroke me with a fist so tight it bordered on painful. Just as my balls drew up, ready to unload in his hand, Xan let loose of my length and pushed a hand against my back until I was face down on the cushion, ass high and spread wide.

Without the use of my hands, I was slightly off balance. Xan smacked a hand against my ass so hard that I yelped. "You don't come until your ass is dripping my cum." He gripped my hips, digging his fingers in so hard I knew there'd be marks, and began to pound into my ass. The sound of flesh slapping against flesh mixed on the air with Xan's grunts and my whimpery moans. A few of his thrusts took my breath away.

"Please, Xan, need to come," I begged.

"Not until I fill this greedy ass with all my cum," Xan growled and slapped me hard enough I could almost picture how hot his handprint would look on my pale skin. With three more forceful thrusts, Xan froze, his dick buried balls deep, and roared as he exploded.

I groaned as his throbbing cock stretched me and painted my channel with hot cum. I cried out when Xan pulled from me, desperate to keep him inside. Xan hauled me to my back, my arms still wrenched behind me, and laid beside me. Within seconds, my ass was filled with Xan's fingers.

"Love watching my cum drip from your ass." Xan's

fingers scooped sticky moisture from my skin and pressed it back into my hole before taking my cock deep into his throat.

After sucking me deep and finger fucking my sensitive ass, Xan popped off. "Need you to come, want to feel your ass clench on my fingers while you pour your cum down my throat."

When Xan teased my prostate, I thrust my hips up and shot into his waiting mouth as he swallowed every last drop. All too soon, my ass was empty, my sensitive cock softening, and the cum leaking from my ass was just a sticky mess.

But, *holy shit*. "That was fucking amazing," I mumbled. "But my arms are starting to hurt."

"Shit, I forgot about your arms." Xan scrambled to untie me.

I immediately wrapped my arms around Xan and nuzzled into his chest. "Thank you for that. So good. Was it okay?"

"Definitely not a hardship," Xan teased and kissed the top of my head. "You like me slapping your ass, definitely good information for the future."

"I liked everything you did." I shifted in his arms.

"Not too sore?" Xan ran a hand down my back.

"Not too bad. Can we shower and move to the bed?" I was definitely feeling sticky and gross.

We spent the next several minutes in the shower soaping each other with soft, slow hands and gentle kisses peppered among sweet words. By the time we crawled into bed, my eyes were nearly impossible to keep open.

"Thank you for tonight. Not sure why I needed that,

but it was amazing." I curled into Xan's chest as his arm came around me.

"I'm happy to give you anything and everything you need," Xan whispered.

"Never knew I needed you. Turns out you're the one thing I needed the most."

"Same." He kissed the top of my head. "I love you."

"Love you," I mumbled.

A slight worry filled me when I thought of Chrome contacting Xan, but Xan pulled me close and I slipped into a peaceful sleep.

\* \* \*

The next morning, I walked into Rose Gardens with Ginny's favorite coffee and donuts.

"Ah, just the pick-me-up I needed today," Ginny exclaimed when she opened her door and ushered me inside.

"You feeling bad again?" My heart lurched.

"No, just in a grumpy mood. But coffee and donuts make it better."

"And your favorite nephew, right?" I winked as I spread out our breakfast on the small table.

"Of course, that's just a given." Ginny turned the little space heater on under the table. "If that gets too hot on you, let me know. My feet are freezing."

I knew my feet would be sweating by the time I left, but I wouldn't make her turn it off. She was more sensitive to temperatures lately.

"What brings you by?" Ginny breathed in deeply from her coffee cup.

"I can't just come visit and bring treats?" I took a bite of the sugary donut.

"You *can*," she began.

"And I often do," I interrupted, enjoying our teasing banter.

"But it feels like you've got something on your mind." Ginny nibbled at a donut and closed her eyes. "These are perfection."

"You all of a sudden a mind reader?"

"Tell me I'm wrong."

I sighed. "Okay, you're completely right." I ate the rest of the donut and grabbed another one.

"Glad you brought a whole box since you look like you're eating your feelings. Save some for me." Ginny pulled the box closer to her side of the table. "Tell me what's wrong."

I sipped my coffee. "It's Xan."

Ginny's brows raised. "Trouble in paradise already?"

"Maybe? Kinda? I don't know." I ran a hand over my short hair.

"Talk to me." Ginny made a *come on* gesture.

"So, I know he was involved in several motorcycle clubs growing up. He did errands for them, ran products —which he later realized were likely drugs—stole parts from rival clubs. They used him in fights and made money off him. They also pimped him out to any women willing to pay." My eyes grew wide. "And I definitely shouldn't be telling you any of this. Please, keep this confidential."

Ginny nodded. "Always. I'll take the details to my grave." She smiled sadly. "Sooner rather than later."

"Stop that, don't be maudlin."

Ginny waved away my comment. "I knew the kid had

had a rough past, just didn't know the extent. Makes me all the happier to know you've both found each other." She frowned. "I thought things were looking good with you? Seemed pretty fiery at the party."

My cheeks heated. "I guess we've just hit our first bump." I took another bite, washed it down, and continued. "One of his old leaders came to visit. Wants Xan to do something for him. I'm bothered that this guy tracked him down. I don't think Xan kept his whereabouts updated with old clubs. I'm also concerned about him getting involved with them again." I leaned forward to rest my head in my hands. "I'm the most upset that Xan started out trying to hide it from me. He's told me a bit more now that I've pushed, but he's not telling me everything."

Ginny took another bite of her first donut while I started on my third. "Yeah, I can see all of your concerns being valid. But it also seems like Xan is a smart guy. Maybe he needs some time to process. He's likely not adjusted to the fact that he has friends to turn to when faced with a predicament. I'd say give him a bit to work it out before you're hurt that he hasn't told you everything."

"And if he never tells me everything? Or this starts to be something that happens a lot?" I knew the answer even though I didn't want to think about it.

Ginny cocked her head to the side. "Then you admit you—and the rest of us—completely misjudged him and you cut your losses. You don't deserve to be lied to or kept in the dark." She patted my hand. "But don't jump to hasty conclusions or make rash decisions just yet. Keep the communication open. Let him know you support him. That's all you can do."

"That's pretty much what Bode said, too." I popped the last bite of donut in my mouth.

"Oh, so the old lady is your second choice for advice. I see." She crossed her arms and attempted to frown.

I chuckled. "No, Bode noticed something was wrong at dinner and asked me about it. But hearing the same advice from both of you is helpful."

We chatted for a bit longer. Ginny had a big day of games, book club, and painting set up. I headed out when it was time for her physical therapy. She gave me a hug and kissed my cheek.

"I think you and Xan are very good for each other. I haven't known the adult Chase for very long, but I know that you're much happier and seem more complete than that first day you came here to see me. I'm sure that has a lot to do with Rosie, the Silvers, your job, and all of that. But I can't help but think Xan plays a very large part. Give him a chance to make things right." She patted my shoulder.

As I walked to my car, I smiled. Ginny was right. There were *a lot* of new things in my life that had made everything better. But Xan really was that missing piece. Having him in my life allowed me to be real. I'd never realized I wasn't being true to myself until I met Xan. And I wasn't going to let that go without a fight.

# 18

---

## XAN

I PACED MY KITCHEN. Chase was coming over soon. We'd decided to just hang out instead of working on the bike that evening. To be honest, my head wasn't in the rebuild at the moment.

Chase deserved to know what Chrome had said.

But if I told him I was actually considering it, would Chase leave me? Surely he wouldn't stay with someone who would do what Chrome wanted. But, then again, would Chase stay with someone who would let what Chrome was threatening happen?

I growled and ran a hand through my hair as the conversation with Chrome replayed through my head.

*I turned from the vendor with duck food for both kids.*

*"Gotta love feeding the ducks," a voice commented from beside me.*

*My head jerked at the sound and I immediately knew who was there before I even saw Chrome standing there with his evil smile. "What the fuck are you doing here?" I demanded as I threw a glance over my shoulder to make sure Chase, Oliver, and Rosie were still on the other side of the pond.*

*"I've got a deal for you."*

*"Not interested."*

*Chrome clucked his tongue. "Now, now, let's not be hasty. Hear me out. There's good money in it."*

*We'd drifted toward a little grove of trees and I positioned myself so my back was to the pond and hopefully blocking the sight of Chrome in case Chase could see me.*

*"I don't need money." I fought the urge to crush the little edible, biodegradable duck food cups. "You need to leave and don't come back."*

*"Would be a shame if your new-found sexuality was outed to your friends," Chrome mused.*

*I snorted. "That's all you've got? You're going to tell my circle of friends—most of whom are gay—that I've had a bisexual awakening? Fuck off."*

*Chrome sneered. "Then maybe I out your friends. I'm sure there are a lot of people who would take their business elsewhere."*

*My eyes grew wide. Was he actually serious or was he just fucking with my head before he dropped the real threat? "We live on Mass. Ave. There's a very large community of LGBTQIA residents and business owners. I assure you that not a single person is going to give a shit that a bar, a massage therapy spa, or an art studio are run by gay men." I cocked my head. "You kinda suck at this."*

*Chrome's eyes narrowed and I knew the real deal was coming. "Maybe I mess up the adoption of pretty baby Cori."*

*My gut clenched and a cold sweat broke across my skin. How the fuck did he know about Cori?*

*"Yeah, that's more like it. Let the birth mother and her parents*

*know about Kyson and Bay being gay. Wonder how they'd feel that Cori's adoptive parents have an accused drug dealer, rapist, thief, and murderer around their baby? I bet that could cause a real issue with Sage and Bode adopting Rosie as well." Chrome stroked his greasy beard.*

*I was going to puke. How did he know all of my friends and the kids? "I didn't do any of those things and you know it."*

*Chrome shrugged. "Won't matter. All I need is the accusations of the crimes. Those will be damning enough even if you didn't actually do any of the things you're accused of. I've got plenty of high-profile clients who owe me. They'll be glad to make the accusations." He shrugged. "Or you could do this one little favor and I'll disappear. One delivery to our biggest rival and return to the Pit with a package. Then it's over and done. Forever."*

*Bile rose in my throat. "Why me?"*

*"You were involved with both clubs. You'll be the most inconspicuous."*

*My nostrils flared. "Is it illegal?"*

*Chrome threw his head back and laughed. "I guess the better question would be is it worth the risk?"*

*Chrome had given me a week and left me standing with duck food spilling from my shaking hands.*

The buzzer broke into my thoughts.

I buzzed Chase in.

He smiled and raised a take-out bag of Chinese. "Dinner is served." His face fell when he saw me. "What's wrong?"

"Nothing. Let's eat." My heart hurt and my brain was screaming at me to stop pushing Chase away. *You're going to lose him, you damn idiot.*

I attempted to keep up with the small talk Chase was

throwing at me, but I knew I did a piss-poor job. By the time we cleaned up the food, the tension in my apartment was thick.

"I'm going to ask you again to tell me what's going on." Chase backed me into the corner of the kitchen counter and crossed his arms over his chest. "I won't keep asking; I can't give unlimited chances. If you can't turn to me, let me in, trust me, then this relationship isn't built on what I thought it was."

My anger and confusion and fear boiled over and I exploded. "You want in on what's going on? Fine! Chrome wants me to make a delivery and bring a package back to the Pit. It's more than likely illegal. If I don't do it, he'll bring accusations against me for drugs, rape, and murder. And then he'll use those accusations and my relationship to the Silvers to mess with Cori's and Rosie's adoptions." My voice was too loud and I wanted to push Chase away. "What do you think about that shit? I either do something illegal and let myself get pulled back into club life after saying I'd *never* go back *or* I become an accused rapist, drug dealer, and murderer along with fucking up the adoptions of two innocent kids and men I've come to love as brothers. How the fuck do I make that decision?" My breathing was fast and my heart thumped quickly in my chest. "How the hell do I make that decision?" I whispered.

Chase pulled me into a tight hug. "That's a lot to take in and deal with."

"How is it even a decision? I can't mess with their happiness." I clung to him as tears stung my eyes.

Chase shook his head. "This is more than we can handle on our own. You need to go to Bode and Bay, tell them what's going on, get their input and let them help."

I shook my head. "And get them involved? Scare them? Disappoint them? I can't."

"So, you're going to do what Chrome is asking?" Chase's eyes were wide, his words incredulous.

"I don't see that I have a choice." I clasped my hands behind my head.

"You always have a choice. It may not be a choice you like, it may be the scarier of the two options, but you have a choice." Chase cupped my face. "You can't go back to your past when you've worked so hard to escape it."

"But if I do what he wants, just this once, it will be over. Truly over. No more worrying about my past coming back to haunt me." My words sounded hollow even to my own ears.

Chase scoffed. "Yeah, I'm sure Chrome will keep his word and leave you alone after you do this *one* thing." He gritted his teeth and closed his eyes. "Listen to yourself Xan. You honestly think that he'll stop with this one thing? Once he knows how to get to you, he'll never stop. He'll own you."

"You don't understand," I started.

Chase pulled away from me and backed toward the door. "You're right, I don't." He shook his head, tears bright in his eyes. "I thought we were forged in truth, respect, and love. If you're willing to do *this*, then we definitely aren't and I can't stand by and watch you go back to a past like that when you know it's wrong." Chase opened the door.

"Even if it means saving people I love?" I was in an impossible and desperate situation.

"Those people you love also love you. Go to them, trust them, let them help." Chase's eyes begged me.

I shook my head. "I don't know how to involve them and ask for their help without putting them at risk."

"Then I can't be here. I love you and I will support you, but that support is only when you're doing the right thing. I can't support illegal activity, even if it's in the name of protecting our friends. You have other options, but you have to reach out for them and be willing to admit you're in a scary situation that you can't fix on your own." Chase walked out. The quiet click of the door was a stake to my heart.

I dropped to my knees. Heaving sobs wracked my body. I cried until I had no more tears. I cried for the little boy I used to be, the one who didn't deserve the hand he was dealt. I cried for the man I was now, the one who didn't know how to fix a desperate situation without hurting either myself or others. I cried for the probable loss of my best friend and boyfriend.

When I had nothing left to cry, I pulled myself up and took a deep breath. Somewhere amongst the tears, I'd come to a decision. I'd worked too hard to get my life together to give it back to the club again. I'd be damned if Chrome was going to own me again.

I needed help and that was okay. I owed it to the Silvers to let them know what was going on. I hated that I'd brought the trouble their way, but was man enough to apologize for that and admit I needed their input and assistance in making this go away.

I was done letting my past control me. I was no longer alone. I had friends, resources, and a reason to stand up for what was right. Arlo, Oliver, Rosie, and Cori—maybe even Chase's and my child one day—deserved someone who did the right thing even if it wasn't the easy thing. And their dads were the ones who could help me do that.

I knew I wouldn't sleep a wink that night, but I was at peace as I waited for the sun to rise.

## 19

---

## CHASE

I WENT DOWN to The Lizard after checking in on Oliver and Rosie.

Bay was at the bar chatting with Bode while Sage flitted around filling drink orders and occasionally popping into their conversation.

"What's wrong with you?" Bode asked as soon as he saw me.

"Xan and I maybe broke up?" I shrugged. "I don't know. He's in trouble, won't ask for help, and I can't be with someone who would do what he's considering."

Bode turned and went to the back. He returned with Ryan. "Need you to man the bar. We'll be at the corner table. Holler if it gets too crazy." Ryan nodded.

Bode filled a pitcher of beer while Sage grabbed four mugs.

Without a word, I followed them to the corner table with Bay close behind me. Once the beers were poured, Bode nodded my way. "Spill it."

I took a long drink from my mug before sighing. "I feel bad talking about his personal shit, but it involves more than just him and I don't think he's doing the right thing." I frowned. "I just don't want you all to think badly of him."

"Just tell us what you can." Sage took my hand.

Without giving *all* the details, because I didn't want to freak the guys out about the kids, I relayed as much of what Xan had told me as I could.

When I finished, we all sat sipping our beers while they thought over what I'd told them.

"Gotta say that I'm disappointed and angry," Bode started.

"But I completely get that he's trying to protect us," Sage interrupted.

"Exactly what I was going to say," Bode shot back.

"He's got to know that doing something illegal isn't going to help anyone in the long run. Chrome won't stop at this one favor," Bay grumbled.

"That's what I told him. I don't know where to go from here, don't know how to help him if he's not willing to help himself." I drank the rest of my beer.

"In the long run, I think we've got to do the same thing I suggested to you the other night at dinner," Bode said. "Give him the time to come to the right answer on his own, let him know we're here to help."

"And if he opts for the illegal activity, both he and we will have to deal with the repercussions of that," Bay added.

No one said anything, but everyone knew that would mean the loss of Xan's job, his apartment, his closeness to the Silvers and their children.

My heart hurt. It would also have to mean the loss of our relationship.

"So, we wait?" I asked.

"I think that's all we can do at this point," Sage said.

"I'm going to text him, let him know we're here for him when he's ready." Bay pulled his phone from his pocket.

Our little group broke up soon after and I carried my heavy heart up the steps. With one last check on the kids, I took a shower and flopped into bed. I already missed Xan as if he'd been cut from my life. I empathized with the impossibility of his predicament—and I hated Chrome for putting Xan in the situation—but, no matter how much I loved him, I couldn't support him doing something illegal. I knew in my heart that Xan would only do the errand for the club because he thought it was the only way to protect Cori and Rosie and the guys. I sent up a little prayer that he'd come to his senses and let the guys help instead of trying to solve the problem on his own.

*And what exactly can the guys even do? How can they fix the situation? Can they keep him from being falsely accused of rape, drug dealing, theft, and murder?*

The pain in my heart and stomach kept me awake most of the night. My brain ran through about five thousand scenarios looking for some sort of answer, but I came up with nothing. How could I demand Xan ask for help when I wasn't sure there was any way to help him in this situation?

By the time the sun rose, I felt as if I was going insane. I was exhausted, I was scared, and I missed Xan. I had absolutely no clue how to fix any of this.

My phone buzzed.
A text.
To the whole crew.
From Xan.


*Xan: Can we all meet somewhere to speak in private?*

## 20

---

## XAN

AT SOME POINT, I must have fallen asleep because I woke to a text from Bay.

*Bay*: *We don't know the whole story, but the guys and I want you to know that we're here for you and are willing to help. Don't attempt to solve this on your own and lose everything you've worked so hard for.*

Even if I hadn't made up my mind last night, Bay's words were a comfort. I took a deep breath and texted the entire crew.

*Me*: *Can we all meet somewhere to speak in private?*

Benji replied that the studio wasn't open until noon and

we were all welcome to meet there. After several texts, it was decided the group would meet at the studio at nine. That gave everyone time to shower. It also gave the parents time to arrange for babysitters. I figured Bonnie, Millie, and Ginny would be happy to help if able; if not, the kids could hang out at the studio and paint.

After a shower, I ran by a bakery and picked up an assortment of pastries before heading to The Silver and Gold Creative. I figured someone else would bring beverages or maybe Benji and Rhys would let us use their coffee and tea station.

Chase met me at the door to help with the box and bags I struggled to balance. I followed him to the little sitting area and put down the pastries. He and I faced each other and stared awkwardly for a brief moment. His face was filled with uncertainty and hopeful anticipation. I closed the gap between us and took him in my arms.

"I'm done letting my past control me. Thank you for making me see that I have other choices. I don't know how to fix this and I can't do it on my own." I held him tight and kissed the side of his head.

Chase relaxed and shuddered in my arms. "Thank you," he whispered. "I don't want to lose you."

"Not going anywhere."

"Okay," Bode's voice boomed. "Tell me there's food and coffee."

Sage and Bode walked across the sales floor hand-in-hand.

"Found someone for the kids?" Chase asked.

"Yeah, Ginny was glad to help with them. Picked her up, took all three over to Bay's place. Millie and Bonnie were already there. Worked out perfectly." Sage kissed Chase's cheek. "You okay?"

From his place in my arms, Chase nodded. "I am now. I will be."

Bay and Kyson arrived just as Rhys was placing little paper plates next to the pastries. Kyson held one beverage holder while Bay balanced a second.

"Tell me one of those is a black coffee," Bode demanded.

"Yes, dear, black like your soul," Bay teased.

"Four black coffees, two mocha lattes, and two chai teas." Kyson placed his carrier on the table.

For about five minutes, we gathered food, sorted beverages, and settled in. Once all eight of us were seated in the tiny area, I quickly polished off half of a croissant and took a fortifying drink of coffee.

Bay held up his hand. "Let's just enjoy our breakfasts for a moment. You don't have to rush."

I nodded gratefully before eating the other half of the pastry and slowly sipping the rich, black coffee.

Several moments later, Bode glanced around. "Okay, we've fed the beasts and caffeinated them, you should be good to speak now."

I launched into the fully-detailed story of Chrome coming to find me, how he knew information about all of them, his ridiculous threats, and then the actual threat he made toward me and the adoptions. The words poured from me and I wondered briefly if I'd stopped breathing as I spoke. Chase's hand on mine grounded me. When I reached the end of the story, I took a deep breath and fought the lump in my throat.

"I'm so sorry. At first, I thought I could do what

Chrome wanted, but I realized I can't let my past control me. I feel trapped and I need help." I lifted my eyes for the first time and made eye contact with each man.

My heart clenched when I recognized nothing but love and support in their faces. The fear I'd been holding onto that told me they'd fire me, kick me out, turn their backs on me melted away.

We sat in silence for a few moments while each man processed the words I'd shared.

Eventually, Bode broke the silence. "Is Chrome very smart?"

I thought about the question. "He's evil and cunning, but he's way too impressed with himself and his power to be super smart. Why?"

"Well, that works in our favor. All of it." Bode steepled his fingers under his chin.

"What are you thinking?" Sage asked.

Over the next hour, we brainstormed ideas, mapped out a plan, and hashed out specific details. In the end, we came up with the plan. It wasn't fool-proof, but it was good and it was all we had.

"I can have my pieces in place in two days." Bode picked up his phone and started tapping out a message. "Bay, what about you? Two days enough?"

Bay nodded.

"Xan, contact Chrome tomorrow. Tell him you've made your decision. Ask him to meet you in front of Whitfield's the next day." Bode crossed his arms over his chest. "That prick is going to learn not to mess with one of us."

\* \* \*

Two days later, I was a thousand percent sure the plan was ridiculous and wouldn't work. But I stood in front of Whitfield's with Bay. The guys were just inside. Bode's police officer friend, Mark, and the Silvers' lawyer, Darron, were also there and listening.

"You ready for this?" Bay asked.

I nodded. "As ready as I'll ever be."

The roar of Chrome's Chopper rumbled down the street.

"Buck up, don't let him see you're scared." Bay crossed his arms over his chest. The bug was buried under the collar of his leather jacket.

I crossed my arms and attempted to look like I didn't give a fuck.

It was the farthest thing from the truth, but it was my only option right then. I had to fix this, protect the kids, and save what Chase and I had.

Chrome narrowed his eyes as he approached from where he'd parked across the street. With a smarmy grin, he joined us on the sidewalk. "Well, well, well, I thought you had an answer for me, Xander. I didn't know you were bringing your daddy to fight for you."

Bay ignored the jab and stuck out his hand. "Good to see you again, Chrome. I won't take up much of your time, but I wouldn't be a very good friend or boss if I didn't attempt to sway you from what you're asking Xan to do."

Chrome rolled his eyes and gestured in a *go on* manner. "Let's get it over with, I've got places to be."

I wondered briefly if Chrome had been staying in town or driving back and forth between states.

"Listen, we're in similar businesses, I was hoping we could be professional about this. Xan has worked hard to build a new life. What would it take to get you to leave him out of your plans and find another runner?" Bay asked.

Chrome sucked on his teeth. "Now see, I'm not sure I can do that. Xander has an in with both clubs and wouldn't look suspicious."

Bay's jaw tightened even though we'd been prepared for Chrome to *not* cooperate. "Xan, can you give us a moment?" Bay nodded toward the door.

His request took me off guard a bit, but I walked into the shop. I knew I'd be able to hear the conversation with the rest of the crew.

"Chrome, I gotta level with you. I don't give a damn if that kid does your dirty work. What I *do* care about is my family." Bay's words were low but exceptionally clear inside the shop.

My heart plummeted.

Bode clapped a hand on my back and Chase took my hand.

"He's acting. He went a bit off script because he felt Chrome wasn't going to talk with our original plan. Don't take any of what he says seriously," Kyson assured from beside me.

"Figured as much." Chrome laughed and sounded positively giddy.

"Now, I'm going to need him to believe there's nothing I can do to help."

From the dark-tinted window, I watched Bay throw a thumb over his shoulder.

"What do you need from me?" Chrome asked. "I'll

help you protect your family as long as I get my runner and product."

"He wasn't fully open with what you've got against him, so I'm not really sure what I'm up against here. It's got to be something pretty serious, right? I can't see Xan throwing away what he's got here unless you've got something really good to hold against him," Bay hedged.

Chrome laughed. "So, he didn't even tell you?"

I watched as Chrome leaned close.

"That damn kid somehow lucked out with a squeaky-clean record even after his time with me and other clubs. So, I had to be a little creative. Threatening to out him or any of his friends wasn't enough for him to take the bait. So, I had to go for the big guns. I've got some high-level friends who owe me. They'd be more than happy to accuse our dear Xander of dealing, rape, theft, and even murder. All I have to do is say the word." Chrome chuckled. "Then I use those accusations to mess with the adoptions y'all have in the works."

I saw Chrome's face take on a sheen of fear and he took a step backwards.

"Not that I'd *actually* mess with your adoptions, but Xander doesn't need to know that, ya know what I'm saying?" Chrome laughed nervously.

I watched as Bay pretended to think over the information.

"So, you need Xan to run product for you. Illegal product, likely drugs or stolen goods. If he does this one favor, you'll leave him alone?" Bay asked.

Chrome stuttered over his words, "Yeah, yeah, of course. Just this once."

"And if he doesn't do your errand, you're going to have

false accusations brought against him—the type that could ruin his life—and he thinks you'll use those allegations to mess up our adoptions? Is that right?" Bay asked.

Chrome nodded. "That's the plan. The accusations won't stick, but he only needs to know that I could fuck up those babies' adoptions. That was all it took and he quickly reconsidered my proposition."

From inside the shop, Bode growled. "You hear enough?" he asked Mark and Darron.

The two men finished scribbling notes and nodded.

"Let's go. Xan, you stay behind us. I don't trust this shithead at all." Bode slammed the door open.

Chrome attempted to run when he saw Bode, Benji, and Rhys followed by Kyson, Sage, Chase, and myself all emerge from the shop. Mark and Darron brought up the rear.

Bay grabbed Chrome by the arm. "Where ya goin', Chrome? No need to run off," Bay crooned. "Seems we had a bit of a misunderstanding. Xan is one of us and you're not getting him to do even the smallest of jobs for you. My contacts are *very* far-reaching. Very. I'll see to it that your Pit Vipers are blackballed and on the watch-list of every law enforcement agency within a hundred miles if you even so much as cross into the city limits of Indianapolis again. In fact, I'd suggest avoiding Indiana all together."

Chrome snarled and spat.

"Come on, Chrome, baby, it's a good deal. The other option is that you approach Xan, and my crew of less-than-savory friends will be turned loose on you. I know *a lot* of people who would make *you* look like fucking Pollyanna." Bay twisted Chrome's arm.

Bode stepped forward. "In case those incentives aren't enough, I'd like you to meet Mark and Darron. Mark is a highly respected member of law enforcement; Darron is a high-profile attorney. They both happened to be visiting and overheard the little conversation you and Bay just had."

Chrome's eyes narrowed.

"Oh, did we forget to mention that Bay was wired? Our bad. But no worries, your threats were very clear and easy to understand. We'll make copies for safe-keeping. Mark and Darron already agreed to sign statements as to what they heard. What's it called? Coercion and extortion?" Bode shivered. "Sounds like it would be a bunch of shit for you to deal with. Probably best to just leave and never come back. Good meeting you." Bode slapped Chrome on the back. "Don't ever darken this city with your ugly mug again, ya hear? We're good guys, family men, but we don't stand for anyone fucking with one of us. You'll regret it, trust me."

Chrome yanked away from Bay and Bode and scowled at the entire group. "Looks like you got yourself some guard dogs, Alexander. And all you had to do was suck dick? Impressive. Who knew I could have sold your ass to the highest bidding cock and made bank?" Chrome straightened the collar of his jacket. "I'll leave. No promises I'll stay gone. Guess you'll always have to wonder."

"It's your funeral if you decide to return. Up to you," Bode stated.

I didn't breathe until Chrome was on his bike and roared away.

The whole group turned and walked into the shop.

Chase hugged me tight.

"Man, I'm sorry for that little bit that went off-script. I worried if you were out there, he would read your face when you heard me say what I had to say." Bay pulled me into a hug. "My family *is* the most important to me, and that includes you. Don't you *ever* try to deal with shit on your own again. You've got a whole crew here ready to fight and support." He patted my back. "And we expect your support in return."

I nodded and tried to speak around the emotion in my throat. "You've got it." I turned to the whole group. "Thank you, all of you. I'm sorry I was stupid for a bit. I've never had friends or family to turn to and I didn't know how it worked. Thank you for being patient with me and standing up for me. I'm sorry for any of the crap I brought with me."

"We've all got shit in our past. We stand together." Bode slapped me on the back. "We've got to get the kids and get to The Lizard. Come in for lunch if you want."

Everyone said their good-byes until it was just me and Chase.

"I gotta be at work a little later. You want to be alone or want some company?" Chase asked.

"Company, please." I headed toward the stairs. Once we were upstairs, I locked the door and kicked off my shoes. "Can we just lay down? I'm exhausted."

Chase nodded and took off his shoes before following me.

I shucked my pants, pulled back the covers, and got in

bed before opening my arms to Chase. "Come here, need you."

Chase stripped to his underwear, climbed into the bed and crawled into my arms. "Today was a bit intense. You think Chrome will stay away?"

I shrugged. "I really don't know what to think. Part of me thinks he'll move onto someone easier to push around. Part of me thinks he'll still bring the allegations against me just to fuck with me because he's pissed."

"We'll take it one day at a time." Chase kissed me. "You've got a whole crew on your side now." He pressed his forehead against mine. "I was so scared I was going to lose you. I'm sorry I left like I did. I knew I'd have to leave if you went back to Chrome, but I was trying to figure out any and every way I could work around it. I hated leaving you like that."

I cupped his face. "No, you leaving me alone like that was for the best. Gave me time to think through what was what. I think I had to reach that breaking point before I could come back and fight. Knowing you and the guys were here for me, knowing you were waiting on me to do the right thing, all of that gave me the strength to reach out. Thank you." I kissed him. "Thank you for your friendship. Thank you for your love. Thank you for being the missing piece I didn't even know I was missing. I love you." I brushed another soft kiss against his lips.

Chase sighed into the kiss before breaking away. "Kinda crazy how our pasts are so much the same yet so different. Took us both being at our lowest to find what we needed the most." He kissed me again. "I'm so grateful our paths crossed. I love you."

# EPILOGUE

## Chase

I MOANED and stretched as I pressed my ass against Xan's morning wood. "Good morning. We should get up and get ready. Ginny and Millie will be waiting." I made as if to roll from the bed.

"Not so fast. We've got time." Xan kissed my neck and rocked his hips into my ass before reaching for my dick. After a couple strokes, he whispered, "Unless you don't want to?"

"You don't play fair," I groaned.

"What's not fair? Just want to slide my cock into your ass and pump you full of my cum while I jerk you off. Seems like a win-win to me." He began to move away from me. "But if you don't want it," he paused.

"Get in my ass," I demanded.

Xan teased a finger along my hip to my ass. When he

breached my hole, I gasped and he laughed. "Pre-lubed, love it."

"We fell asleep before a shower last night." I rocked my ass, loving his finger in me. "Another reason we don't have a ton of time. We need to shower."

Xan spit in his palm, slicked his cock, and slid deep into my ass as he lifted my leg. "Fuck, I will never get tired of this ass."

I grunted as he pumped hard and fast. "Just my ass, huh? That's all I am to you?" I teased.

"This cock, too," Xan whispered gruffly as he reached to take me in his fist. "Gonna fill your pretty ass with hot cum, but I want you to come in my hand first." He stroked, teasing his thumb over my slit. "Wanna feel your tight hole clench around my dick, come for me."

Xan's words pushed me over the edge and I shot my load over his fingers.

He brought his sticky hand to my lips as he thrust deep and hard into my ass. "Suck them," he demanded.

I licked my seed from his finger and sucked him deep, swirling my tongue around his digit.

Xan hefted my leg higher, holding tight as he drilled into my body over and over until he tensed and moaned. His cock pulsed and heat filled my ass as Xan trembled behind me.

Once we'd caught our breaths, Xan pulled slowly from my body. "That was amazing. Always so good with you. Love you." He rolled me to face him and wrapped me in his arms for a slow, sensual kiss.

"Showers first then start a load of laundry for these sheets. I'm not sleeping in crunchy, dried cum tonight." I kissed him again. "Love you. Love waking up to your cock."

"Just my cock?" Xan teased.

"Okay, waking up to *you* is pretty great too." I rolled from bed and my ass gave a twinge. "Three rounds of anal the night and morning before I take my aunt on a motorcycle ride was likely very poor planning on my part." I winced. I needed to work the stiffness out of my knee and take some ibuprofen.

Xan stood and took me in his arms. "I'll soothe your battered ass tonight."

"*You're* the reason my ass is so sore." I slapped at his chest, but I couldn't hold back the smile.

"Fingers and tongue only tonight. I'll work you over real good." Xan grabbed my cock. "And I'd be happy to take this tonight. Give your ass a rest and give mine a workout."

"Lord, you're insatiable. Shower. Now." I pushed him away from me.

Somehow, we left Xan's apartment on time.

* * *

Xan and I had been taking the bikes out every day for about a week, but today was special because we were taking Millie and Ginny for a ride. Millie was at Ginny's when we pulled up to Rose Gardens.

Xan and I both cracked up laughing when we climbed from the bikes and removed our helmets. The ladies were standing out front, clad in leather pants, black boots, leather jackets, and mirrored aviator sunglasses. They each had their hair hidden under red bandanas.

"You girls went all out," Xan drawled, "looking *good*."

"If I'm going to die today, I'm going to look hot," Millie quipped.

"No need to be nervous. We're both good riders." I pulled Aunt Ginny into a hug. "Just lean into the corners, don't fight against them. We won't go too far, just going to get outside of town and find a smooth country road to travel."

"Ladies, any questions?" Xan asked.

"Nope, let's ride." Millie headed toward the bikes.

"This brings back memories." Ginny hooked her arm in mine. "The last time I was on a motorcycle, Rose was driving and we ended up in a hidden grove of trees and she stroked a lot more than just the gears." Ginny cackled.

Millie hooted. "The last time I was on a bike, I found myself in the middle of an orgy out in a corn field. A lot of acid was involved, but a good time was definitely had by all. Pretty sure I took more than a few rides that day, if you get my drift."

The women laughed.

Xan and I groaned.

Once we had everyone settled, the four of us spent the next couple hours riding, enjoying the warm breeze and bright sunshine.

By the time we dropped Ginny and Millie off, the women were noticeably tired, but couldn't stop yammering about how much fun they had. Xan and I promised we'd take them out again soon.

"Ready for lunch before your appointment?" Xan waggled his brow.

My stomach plummeted, but I nodded. "Yeah, I know I need to eat, but I'm afraid I'll puke."

We headed to The Salty Lizard and spent the next hour or so laughing and talking with Sage and Bode while we enjoyed lunch. I wanted a few beers, but Xan advised against it.

"You need to be clear headed. Some places won't do it if you're noticeably drunk." Xan wrapped his arm around my shoulders and jostled me. "You're going to do great."

*　*　*

Late in the afternoon, we walked into the tattoo shop and I nearly swallowed my tongue. I'd already filled out the paperwork and worked with Curtis to finalize my design, so all I had to do was wait. And convince myself this was a mistake. And figure out how to sneak out without Xan realizing I was gone.

"Stop making escape plans," Xan commanded and placed a hand on my knee. "You're going to be fine. Tell me again why you decided to get a tattoo."

I took a deep breath. "I watched you face your fears and overcome your past. Seeing that made me realize I could do the same. I know it's just some ink, but it feels like more. It feels like a new start. I've got you, Rosie, new friends, and this tattoo kind of cements all of those things together and reminds me that I'm strong and I can face anything with all of you by my side."

"I love it, and I love you. Show me the design again?" Xan pulled me close.

I pulled out the mock-up Curtis had done for me. An anvil, surrounded by red roses, and a single zinnia laying across the top of the black metal.

"I love that you came up with this on your own, and I

love that it has meaning to you. Tell me what each piece means."

I knew Xan was just distracting me from my nerves, but I took the bait. "Well first, I told Curtis the pieces I wanted and he designed the image. The anvil is a symbol of virtue, bravery, and strength. Those three things apply to me, you, Rosie, Ginny, and the guys. The roses are love and, of course, Rosie. The zinnia has a lot of meanings. Thoughts of friends, endurance, daily remembrance, goodness, lasting affection, and thoughts of an absent friend. So, it's very much for you and me, the guys, but mostly for Ginny. I kinda hate to get it inked before she's gone, but the fact that she loves zinnias, I just had to include it."

Xan squeezed my hand. "I love you. Thank you for being a part of my life and for letting me be a part of this."

I kissed his cheek. "Thank you for being you and making my life make so much more sense. I love you."

The door swung open and Curtis walked out. "Xan, good to see you, man. Chase, you ready?"

I stood and took a deep breath. "Let's do this." I was talking about the tattoo, but with Xan holding my hand and standing by my side, it felt like I was referring to a lot more than just some ink.

* * *

Be sure to grab the next two books in the Forged in the City series!

Hearts Afire- getbook.at/HeartsAfire

Hearts Aflame- getbook.at/HeartsAflame

## ALSO BY A.D. ELLIS

The BJ Boys Series (3 books, small town, big love)

Forever Better Together (friends to lovers)

His Reluctant Cowboy (age gap, opposites attract, cowboy romance)

What Blooms Beneath (LGBT Fantasy romance)

Sawyer

*(this was the first M/M I wrote and you may remember Sawyer and Luke being mentioned in Barrett & Ivan as well as in Ryker & Gavin)*

\* \* \*

Start Something About Him with a **FREE** short story:

(The Beginning https://instafreebie.com/free/84Cxr)

Then continue with the other stand-alone titles in the series (available to read FREE for Kindle Unlimited subscribers):

Bryan & Jase

Brody & Nick

Barrett & Ivan

Braeton & Drew

Ryker & Gavin

Kade & Cameron

Or grab the boxset HERE.

\* \* \*

Plus several other titles:

Devoted (a Something About Him novella)

Saving Us

Stranded Hearts (a short story)

Eli & Gage (a Something About Him short story)

A.D.'s first stories (all male/female except Sawyer which is male/male) are in the Torey Hope and Torey Hope: The Later Years series. Find the 8 book box set HERE or you can find each individual title on Amazon.

For Nicky

Because of Beckett

Christmas in Torey Hope

Loving Josie

Decker

Sawyer

Zach

Kendrick

# ABOUT THE AUTHOR

A.D. Ellis is an Indiana girl, born and raised. She spends much of her time in central Indiana as an instructional coach/teacher in the inner city of Indianapolis, being a mom to two amazing school-aged children, and wondering how she and her husband of almost two decades have managed to not drive each other insane. A lot of her time is also devoted to phone call avoidance and her hatred of cooking.

She loves chocolate, wine, pizza, and naps along with reading and writing romance. These loves don't leave much time for housework, much to the chagrin of her husband. Who would pick cleaning the house over a nap or a good book? She uses any extra time to increase her fluency in sarcasm.

Find all of Ellis' contemporary romance and male/male romance at www.adellisauthor.com

FREE books-- sign up at bit.ly/ADEllisNews for a FREE male/female romance.

Sign up at http://www.subscribepage.com/ADEllisNewsMMRomance for a FREE male/male romance book.

## ACKNOWLEDGMENTS

It's always so hard to write this part because I'm worried I'll forget someone without meaning to.

Readers- you are the reason I write. As long as you continue reading my stories, I'll continue writing them. Thank you for your support.

Bloggers- your support, reviews, and promotion are very much appreciated. Thank you!

My author buddies- I don't know that I could keep doing this without our brainstorm sessions, laughter, road trips, meals, wine, and friendship as my support.

Thank you to my alphas, betas, editors, proofreaders, and ARC readers! Your eyes and input are beyond important to me.

Brett and Gage- as usual, I doubt you even grasp how much your support, input, and friendship mean to me. This author journey has brought many wonderful things into my life, and you both are two of the BEST! I'm blessed to call you friends.

My family and friends- thank you for your love and support, always.